THE **JOURNEY** PRIZE

STORIES

WINNERS OF THE $10,000 JOURNEY PRIZE

1989
Holley Rubinsky for
"Rapid Transits"

1990
Cynthia Flood for "My Father
Took a Cake to France"

1991
Yann Martel for "The Facts
Behind the Helsinki Roccamatios"

1992
Rozena Maart for "No Rosa,
No District Six"

1993
Gayla Reid for
"Sister Doyle's Men"

1994
Melissa Hardy for
"Long Man the River"

1995
Kathryn Woodward for "Of
Marranos and Gilded Angels"

1996
Elyse Gasco for "Can You Wave
Bye Bye, Baby?"

1997 (shared)
Gabriella Goliger for
"Maladies of the Inner Ear"

Anne Simpson for
"Dreaming Snow"

1998
John Brooke for
"The Finer Points of Apples"

1999
Alissa York for "The Back of the
Bear's Mouth"

2000
Timothy Taylor for
"Doves of Townsend"

2001
Kevin Armstrong for
"The Cane Field"

2002
Jocelyn Brown for
"Miss Canada"

2003
Jessica Grant for
"My Husband's Jump"

2004
Devin Krukoff for
"The Last Spark"

2005
Matt Shaw for "Matchbook for a
Mother's Hair"

2006
Heather Birrell for
"BriannaSusannaAlana"

2007
Craig Boyko for
"OZY"

2008
Saleema Nawaz for
"My Three Girls"

2009
Yasuko Thanh for
"Floating Like the Dead"

THE BEST OF CANADA'S NEW WRITERS
THE **JOURNEY** PRIZE

STORIES

SELECTED BY
PASHA **MALLA**
JOAN **THOMAS**
ALISSA **YORK**

EMBLEM
McClelland & Stewart

A cataloguing record for this publication is available from Library and Archives Canada.

We acknowledge the financial support of the Government of Canada through the Book Publishing Industry Development Program and that of the Government of Ontario through the Ontario Media Development Corporation's Ontario Book Initiative. We further acknowledge the support of the Canada Council for the Arts and the Ontario Arts Council for our publishing program.

"Serial Love" © Carolyn Black; "Confluence of Spoors" © Andrew Boden; "The Dead Dad Game" © Laura Boudreau; "Uncle Oscar" © Devon Code; "Publicity" © Danielle Egan; "The Longitude of Okay" © Krista Foss; "Mating" © Lynne Kutsukake; "When in the Field with Her at His Back" © Ben Lof; "Eat Fist!" © Andrew MacDonald; "Ship's Log" © Eliza Robertson; "Five Pounds Short and Apologies to Nelson Algren" © Mike Spry; "Laud We the Gods" © Damian Tarnopolsky.

Published simultaneously in the United States of America by McClelland & Stewart Ltd., P.O. Box 1030, Plattsburgh, New York 12901

Library of Congress Control Number: 2010923465

Typeset in Janson by M&S, Toronto
Printed and bound in Canada

This book was produced using ancient-forest friendly papers.

McClelland & Stewart Ltd.
75 Sherbourne Street
Toronto, Ontario
M5A 2P9
www.mcclelland.com

1   2   3   4   5   14 13 12 11 10

The $10,000 Journey Prize is awarded annually to an emerging writer of distinction. This award, now in its twenty-second year, and given for the tenth time in association with the Writers' Trust of Canada as the Writers' Trust of Canada/McClelland & Stewart Journey Prize, is made possible by James A. Michener's generous donation of his Canadian royalty earnings from his novel *Journey*, published by McClelland & Stewart in 1988. The Journey Prize itself is the most significant monetary award given in Canada to a developing writer for a short story or excerpt from a fiction work in progress. The winner of this year's Journey Prize will be selected from among the twelve stories in this book.

The Journey Prize Stories has established itself as the most prestigious annual fiction anthology in the country, introducing readers to the finest new literary writers from coast to coast for more than two decades. It has become a who's who of up-and-coming writers, and many of the authors who have appeared in the anthology's pages have gone on to distinguish themselves with collections of short stories, novels, and literary awards. The anthology comprises a selection from submissions made by the editors of literary journals from across the country, who have chosen what, in their view, is the most exciting writing in English that they have published in the previous year. In recognition of the vital role journals play in fostering literary voices, McClelland & Stewart makes its own award of $2,000 to the journal that originally published and submitted the winning entry.

This year the selection jury comprised three award-winning writers:

Pasha Malla's debut collection of stories, *The Withdrawal Method*, won the Trillium Book Award and the Danuta Gleed Literary Award, was shortlisted for the Commonwealth Writers' Prize for Best First Book (Canada/Caribbean), and was longlisted for the Scotiabank Giller Prize. He is also the author of a collection of poetry, *All our grandfathers are ghosts*. A two-time Journey Prize finalist, he lives in Toronto and teaches in the University of Toronto's Department of Continuing Studies. His first novel, *People Park*, will be published in 2011.

Joan Thomas's first novel, *Reading by Lightning*, won the Commonwealth Writers' Prize for Best First Book (Canada/Caribbean) and the Amazon First Novel Award. Her second novel is *Curiosity*. Joan was a long time contributing reviewer for the *Globe and Mail* and co-edited the anthology *Turn of the Story: Canadian Short Fiction on the Eve of the Millennium*. She lives in Winnipeg. For more information, please visit www.joanthomas.ca.

Alissa York's novels include *Mercy*, *Effigy*, which was shortlisted for the Scotiabank Giller Prize, and, most recently, *Fauna*. She is also the author of a collection of short fiction, *Any Given Power*. Her stories have won the Bronwen Wallace Award and the Journey Prize, and have appeared in various literary journals and anthologies. She has lived all over Canada, and now makes her home in Toronto. For more information, please visit www.alissayork.com.

The jury read a total of seventy-four submissions without knowing the names of the authors or those of the journals in which the stories originally appeared. McClelland & Stewart would like to thank the jury for their efforts in selecting this year's anthology and, ultimately, the winner of this year's Journey Prize.

McClelland & Stewart would also like to acknowledge the continuing enthusiastic support of writers, literary journal editors, and the public in the common celebration of new voices in Canadian fiction.

For more information about *The Journey Prize Stories*, please consult our website: www.mcclelland.com/jps.

CONTENTS

READING THE 2010 JOURNEY PRIZE STORIES

A CONVERSATION WITH PASHA MALLA,
JOAN THOMAS, AND ALISSA YORK

ALISSA YORK: There's so much to say about the jurying process. It was an intense, immersive experience, reading and evaluating all those diverse narratives; at times my mind swam with characters and settings, images and events. In the end, though, I believe we all zeroed in on those stories that really stayed with us – the ones that not only moved into our hearts and minds, but stuck around to unpack.

JOAN THOMAS: When you think about it, all we read was the equivalent in pages of two or three novels – and yet there were all those separate imagined worlds to enter. The writer of a short story has so few pages to set up the rules of the game and then play it out. I found I had to do my reading in short sessions to really savour the concentrated force of each story.

PASHA MALLA: One thing I think we were all looking for was to be surprised. And I hope readers of this anthology will find surprises – whether in language, structure, voice, emotional oomph, or in the unexpected twists and turns of a well-told story.

AY: Absolutely – good fiction surprises us the way life does, which is odd, given how easily a story can fail by sticking to "what really happened." I find the sweetest surprises are often the small ones, such as the moment in Lynne Kutsukake's

"Mating" when the protagonist focuses on the whorl of greying hair at the crown of his wife's head and feels "an inexplicable tenderness for this secret spot, a sudden urge to protect it with the palm of his hand." Nothing like getting swept up in a character's unexpected rush of love.

JT: It was remarkable to see what different stories two writers could produce on similar subjects – in the case of "Mating" and Carolyn Black's "Serial Love," a subject as specific as *speed dating*. "Mating" beautifully juxtaposes traditional Japanese cultural attitudes with contemporary dating practices, and "Serial Love" listens in on a first encounter between a man and woman and reveals menace in every word and gesture. It's a story of such precisely balanced ambiguity that its possibilities surprise you with every reading.

PM: And then there were those stories that grab you by the throat from the first line. From their cracking openings on, every sentence of Damian Tarnopolsky's "Laud We the Gods" and Mike Spry's "Five Pounds Short and Apologies to Nelson Algren" is visceral, unsettling, uncompromising, and astonishing. Both are told in the sort of voice that needles its way into your brain and stays with you long after the story is over.

JT: I've come around to thinking that point of view is everything, how fully you inhabit it. Devon Code's "Uncle Oscar," for example, pleased me with every detail that fell under the alert eye of the thirteen-year-old protagonist: the upside-down milk crate that served as a footstool in the basement TV room, a Sepultura T-shirt and an Ibanez guitar, the smell of the unbathed uncle ("a sweet smell like brown bananas") – it's Leo's eye on ordinary stuff that aligns us entirely with his experience.

AY: Yes, and those same details often serve as evidence of an original mind at work. Among others, I'm thinking here of "The Dead Dad Game" by Laura Boudreau and "Ship's Log" by Eliza Robertson, both of which deliver fresh, even startling, takes on the popular theme of childhood loss and grief.

PM: I think that sort of originality is what really set these twelve stories apart from the rest of the pack – which is saying something, as I don't think there was a single one of the seventy-four submissions that wasn't a solid, well-crafted piece of writing.

AY: I love the fact that the search for the "best writing" led us to such diverse styles: the mad aria of "Laud We the Gods" at one end of the spectrum; the haunting plainsong of Andrew Boden's "Confluence of Spoors" at the other. So different from one another and so perfectly themselves.

JT: And, of course, to diverse worlds – it's always a small miracle to find a world created whole within a short story. I was especially struck by writers who used settings we know and managed to disorient us by peeling back that sense of the familiar. "Confluence of Spoors" did it in a stroke, as a hunter follows a trail of blood into Vancouver's East Side. Danielle Egan's "Publicity" did it too, giving us a barely futuristic and surreal Vancouver.

PM: "Confluence of Spoors" is a good example of a story, too, that deserves and benefits from repeat readings. To me that's the mark of a truly strong piece of short fiction: something that engages on the surface, but then, when you go back to it a second (and third) time, gets richer, more nuanced and layered. I feel the same way about "Ship's Log," which is immediately captivating and charming, but sneaks up on you emotionally; you finish, gutted, and want to go back and figure out what was really going on the whole time.

JT: Then of course there was our conversation the day the jury met to discuss the stories, which opened up all sorts of new meanings in the stories. "When in the Field with Her at His Back" is one of the stories that I thought especially rewards a second look. You're aware of the buried past as a diplomat returns to postwar Eastern Croatia to look for an old lover. Revisiting this story, I realized how skilfully Ben Lof had knit his characters' lives together through the image of unexploded landmines.

AY: I agree, the landmines worked beautifully – a perfect underlying symbol for a story about the fragmented, dissociative state so many suffer in the wake of war. I'm fascinated by the power of well-chosen objects in many of these narratives: the soggy picture of Marilyn Monroe in Andrew MacDonald's coming-of-age piece, "Eat Fist!" ("I find her pulpy corpse floating in the drinking fountain."); the perfectly creepy Curious George poster in "Five Pounds Short and Apologies to Nelson Algren." And Pasha, I remember you brought up the impact of the tights-as-tourniquet in "The Longitude of Okay" by Krista Foss – devastating!

PM: Yeah, and also, in the same story, the belt used to secure the classroom door – there's such power in the dramatic repurposing of everyday objects, imbuing them with sudden, unexpected narrative and emotional resonance. That sort of thing always sticks with me, and maybe speaks more broadly to what I often love in fiction: seeing the familiar cast in a new light.

JT: What moved me most about "The Longitude of Okay" were Krista Foss's characters. This story, about a school shooting, could so easily have been contained and prescribed by its subject, but it became instead an insightful exploration of the teacher's self-doubt. And the students are deftly drawn in a few strokes. They're so real.

PM: The last thing I wanted to mention, and which we haven't touched on, was humour. Being funny is so hard to do well, as it relies so much on surprising the reader, and "Uncle Oscar" and "Serial Love" have some killer lines that totally cracked me up. Devon Code's thirteen-year-old narrator imagining cocaine to "feel like taking 500 dumps all at once" is so perfectly hilarious, and I laughed out loud a number of times at Carolyn Black's wonderfully dry descriptions of speed dating.

AY: So often those moments that make us laugh (or cry, for that matter) occur when the writer has hit the nail on the head, getting a character's voice, thought, or action exactly right. It's perhaps the fundamental challenge of writing convincing, compelling fiction, this business of spinning people out of the air – a challenge that the contributors to this year's edition of *The Journey Prize Stories* meet and exceed with style.

THE **JOURNEY** PRIZE

STORIES

CAROLYN BLACK

SERIAL LOVE

Number 29 is talking about serial killers.

Number 14 squints at him across the table. Her squint is a mean, suspicious wrinkle.

"Yes," she thinks.

"No," she thinks.

Unlike other men in the nightclub – men wearing loose-knit sweaters or brightly coloured dress shirts – Number 29 wears a black dress shirt with silver pinstripes. His black pants have creases ironed down the legs. Underneath the closely shorn stubble of his hair, his head looks uneven, dented in the middle and protruding on the right side. "Bullheaded," she thinks, as he blunders on in speech. She writes "bullheaded" down on her scorecard in jagged cursive, so she will remember later that he frightens her.

Number 29 has said that he works as a criminologist. She has said that she works as an indexer.

He has said he is thirty-two. She has said she is thirty-three.

All this may be true.

They have eight minutes to decide.

Already, Number 14 has decided that working as a criminologist is not the only way a man might learn about the behaviour of killers and rapists.

She studies the man across from her. While he speaks, his hands chop at the tabletop in unison, as though he holds a box between them and is shaking it at her. His box of facts and knowledge.

He says, "Do you know what an area of awareness is?"

She shakes her head.

"It's where perpetrators commit most of their crimes and where they feel comfortable, often where they travel between work and home and social events."

"What you're saying is that people commit crimes in areas that mean something to them? Near the people closest to them?"

"It's not my opinion. It's just the way it is."

"Why?"

He eyes the doorway of the club.

"For one thing, it's easier to commit a crime if you know where the escape routes are."

Escape is important for both perpetrators and victims, she thinks. Sometimes it must be hard to tell them apart when they're fleeing the scene.

"For another thing –" he continues and offers her a tentative smile, suddenly ducking his bulky head as though shy. Then he stops smiling and his hands fall onto the table. One flutters, with surprising delicacy, to his jacket pocket and retrieves a pair of wire-rimmed glasses. When he puts them on, she cannot see his eyes.

"For another thing, everyone needs some sense of security."

All evening, the strange men have passed in front of her. No sooner does a man sit down at her table than a bell is rung and he is up and off. After a while, it seems as though these are not different men, but one man who keeps changing his clothes and manner. A man in disguise. It is hard not to be suspicious of such a man – a man who keeps altering, like the landscape of the city, which is always under construction and covered with scaffolding, always getting torn down and rebuilt. Just as she adjusts to one view of the city, the next thing she knows, everything has changed. The buildings have gone from small to large or large to small and the familiar people are gone and unfamiliar people are in their place.

The nightclub has been built from stainless steel – bar, bar stools, walls, and low tables – as though designed to withstand crowds of people flowing through on their way to elsewhere. It reminds her of a subway station.

Two men before the criminologist, she meets a man who looks like a country singer, with his cowboy boots and square, bearded jaw, and when she asks him if this is what he does, he shouts, "Why does everyone keep asking me that!" He reminds her of her fourth boyfriend, who always shouted at her with reproach, so she ticks No on her scorecard. One man before the criminologist, she meets a man who owns a distribution business, but he will not tell her what he distributes. His silver rings remind her of the rings her sixth boyfriend used to twist around his fingers while crying over her indifference to his feelings, so she ticks No on her scorecard.

No, no, no. It begins to feel like indexing, breaking each man down into parts, then putting the parts into categories. When she was younger, the world was broad and unknown. Now, she knows that world so well she can divide it up into index cards, which prevent her from making the same mistakes twice.

Number 29 holds a clear drink, a lime slice pinching the side of the glass. It looks like a gin and tonic.

She says, "That's what my eighth boyfriend used to drink. I thought he'd drunk them all. I thought there were none left in the world, he was so thirsty."

Number 29 laughs, barkingly, but by the time she thinks to laugh, he has stopped.

"Ah, my ex-girlfriend was also sarcastic," he smiles, but then looks away. "She was sarcastic even while she was leaving our apartment for the last time and getting into a car with another man. Even then she still thought she had some right to sarcasm."

He leans back in his chair and eyes her across the table.

The bell will ring soon. Their time is almost up.

"I'm a feminist," she says. She brandishes the word as though laying down something between them, a bundle board in a bed, for instance.

"Yes, so was my ex-girlfriend. I could be friends with a feminist," he says.

Already, they are building their escape hatches, so when it comes time to flee the scene – and it will come, she thinks, staring at his shirt – the getaway will be fast and easy.

———

But! His hands have begun to dance out a new choreography. Now as he speaks, instead of chopping at the air, he dabbles with his fingers across the table as though laying out his words in rows. This seems familiar. This seems like what she does with words while arranging an index. Lulled by his dainty dabbles, she finds the chopping motion less violent and more generous when it returns. As he holds out his box of air to her again, she feels he may be offering her some intangible gift.

She throws one of her legs over the other and shifts both out from under the table, swinging her foot beside him. Then she remembers she knows nothing about him and sweeps her legs back under the table. Above the table, only her high-necked sweater is visible. Under the table, her black skirt barely covers her thighs.

She is thinking about areas of awareness, the familiar spaces where criminals commit their crimes.

"What about with bodies?"

He looks confused, so she traces the space around her hand, saying, "This is my area of awareness. But when I move my hand beside yours into your area of awareness –" she lays her hand beside his on the tabletop, so her thumb is milli-metres from his own, " . . . whose area is it? Who is the more likely perpetrator when two areas overlap?"

Deviancy is an odd thing to flirt about, but he is smiling.

"That's not criminal theory, the body as an area of aware-ness," he says. "That's a theory of something else you're working on." His smile widens, and this time her squint relaxes and she allows herself to grimace in amusement.

They lean closer together.

Yes. Yes. Yes.

The bell.

After Number 14 meets six more men, the bell rings for the last time and she tears the white sticker from her sweater. The sticker has a one and four written in pink marker, no name. She leaves it crumpled on the bar and drops her scorecard into the slot of a box wrapped in silver paper with red hearts. She has checked Yes beside only one number – his number.

As she walks past him on her way to the washroom, he touches her lower back, fanning his fingers across her spine. Her body is in love. It has fallen in love in three seconds. With a hand. Of course, it could be the hand of a serial killer, she thinks, squinting meanly into her eyes in the washroom mirror.

She is wearing four breasts tonight, two real and two padded discs, cupping the real as hands would, as his hands might. As she reaches for the taps, one disc slides towards her neck.

She imagines Number 29's fingers on her breasts, dabbling out their rows. She tries to reason it out. Even if he is a serial killer, perhaps he will not hurt her if she is willing and does not resist. In fact, if she is willing, she might never need to learn that he is a serial killer. This is the bargain she strikes with her reason.

It has been a while since a man touched her back.

She could leave the washroom and go home. The event is over. In a few days, if he has checked Yes beside her number on his scorecard, she will be sent his e-mail address. When she arrived, she signed a waiver stating she understood attendees were not screened. She released the event's organizers from any responsibility for what followed the final ring of the bell.

Suspicion lurked at the evening's outskirts like a peeping Tom.

"I am willing," she whispers through her teeth, squeezing the taps. "I am willing." Her molars grind together.

She retucks her fourth breast into her bra.

He is sitting at the back of the club on a low, modern sofa, a white rectangle with steel legs. He rubs his index finger against his thumb, staring off into space. The tip of his tongue darts in and out of the corner of his mouth to the rhythm of his rubbing. She decides not to see this. Instead, she sits down beside him.

"So how many women did you pick tonight? How many are you going to see again?"

"Maybe I won't have to see any others," he says.

He offers her his drink.

"About that eighth boyfriend of yours," he says as she takes the glass, "my grandfather was an alcoholic." She sips and tastes only mineral water with lime. He takes back the glass and looks into her eyes. "I don't drink."

"And I'm not always sarcastic," she murmurs.

Over the next two hours, he fills in the details of a life that is placid and unthreatening. He works for the police and his brother teaches at the private boys' school near her apartment. He meets his parents and brother at a pub every Sunday for lunch. He owns a home in the suburbs just outside the city. One of his friends is a fireman.

While he speaks, her body – with preening self-caresses and head tilts – is holding a covert discussion with his. Her body is welcoming his, rolling out its little red carpets while doorkeepers swing wide the doors. She is barely aware of what her body is up to until she notices that she and Number 29 are sandwiched together, her hand on his knee, his arm around her waist. A great strategizer, the body has dumped doses of oxytocin – the body's rohypnol – into her bloodstream to counteract her adrenalin, to relax and stun her.

They leave the restaurant. Night has shrouded the streets and alleys. As Number 29 steps onto the sidewalk, night falls over his head and shoulders like a black hood.

He turns to face her, where she stands in the doorway, and holds out his hand.

"Come on. I'll drive you home." With his other hand, he scoops a key ring from his trenchcoat pocket and whirls it around one finger – more confidence than he has shown all night.

His keys. His car. His area of awareness.

In the parking garage, he mentions that hidden eyes are watching her.

"Security cameras," he says, scanning the concrete roof.

She trails behind him as he points at beige cones poking from the ceiling like tiny beehives. She always thought they were sprinklers.

She thinks about getting into his car.

Yes.

No.

"This is a high-risk society," he says, still looking up. "Terrorism, bio-chemical warfare . . ."

" . . . HIV, hepatitis, pregnancy, serial killers," she thinks.

"I have a camera for a brain. I remember everything about tonight."

"What do you mean?"

"Sitting at the table beside yours was Number 26, a lawyer in jeans and a green sweater. Beside her was Number 10, gold barrette and contact lenses. I saw the rings around her irises. Then Number 12, picked at one of her cuticles the whole time we talked. Black wool skirt, run in her nylons. Then Numbers 20 and 18 and 4. And on the other side of the bar, 8, 16, 2, 22, 30, 6, 28, and 24. I could tell you how each woman dressed and how she behaved and what she said. Five women wore glasses and only two wore jeans. Nine worked as teachers. And you, you were Number 14."

Number 14 stops walking.

"I think I'll take the subway home."

He stops as well and turns to face her. "Why? Are you nervous about me seeing your place? Are you married?" He pretends to joke but his voice cracks on the final word.

The problem with his questions is this: she cannot answer them. She cannot say, "I suspect you might be a serial killer," for if he turns out not to be a serial killer, such a statement is an insult, and if he turns out not to be a serial killer, she might want to see him again.

He takes off his glasses and blinks down at her, as though he is just as confused as she is. Then he reaches forward and lays a large hand on her arm.

She sees this image – his hand on her arm – as though watching it from above her own body. She imagines police officers in a dank concrete room, viewing the security video from tonight, clearing their throats, taking notes.

She asks Number 29, "Do you wear a uniform?"

"I don't follow."

"At your job, do you wear a uniform?"

He steps back from her and takes his hand off her arm.

"No. Sorry. Women always ask me that. I'm sure I could rent one if you wanted."

He turns away from her and moves between two parked cars, saying over his shoulder, "People used to focus on punishing criminals once a crime had been committed, but these days we try to prevent crimes before they happen."

He opens the passenger door of a black hatchback and looks at her expectantly.

"Of course, security is all a question of balance," he says. "Balancing caution against necessary risk. There are no guarantees."

There are no guarantees. But there are safeguards.

"Just a minute," she says and pulls her cellphone from her jacket. "I need to check my messages."

While he fiddles with his own cellphone, she lowers hers and snaps a photo of the back of his car.

Then she texts a co-worker, someone who might ask questions if Number 14 stopped showing up for work.

"I met someone!!!"

She attaches this message to the photo of his licence plate and hits send.

"Don't let them take you to a second location," she remembers a newscaster saying about serial killers, as she slides into his car. "That's where they kill you."

No.

Yes.

She pulls shut the door.

———

They drive away from the city centre, travelling north up a highway and then a series of side streets. She does not drive and is unfamiliar with this route to her apartment, but he knows the area. His brother lives nearby, he says.

The car has leather seats and a CD changer in the back. She has never heard, before now, of a CD changer. He widens his eyes with disbelief and pleasure at such naivete. As a female folk singer wails through the car's speakers, he grins about all the things he knows.

"Have you ever seen the houses along Arbour Path?" he asks.

When she shakes her head, he announces, "I'll take you for a drive then."

He turns down more and more streets, away from the street lights and into a residential area thick with trees. She sways with the car, relaxed and dizzy.

High walls of stone and tightly packed evergreens, as well as wrought-iron security gates with cameras and intercoms, surround the houses. A jeep with the words "Securo-Guard" written on one side cruises past. The houses look like sets from a movie. Massive Greek columns glow in the dark. Spotlights shine on the arched stone entrances of Tudor manors. These homes are not like anything an architect would design for beauty, but like something the owners imagined would be a grand home when they were ten years old. Number 14 stares at a stucco Italian villa and realizes that it is not a house but merely a dream of a house.

Number 29 points out five-car garages. He talks about what sort of house he might like to live in. What sort of house he has now. How many children it would take to fill his house (one) and how many children before he would have to move (two). He lays it all out like a banking plan. His voice drones on, nasally, but she is not paying attention. She is watching his large hands grip the steering wheel.

The houses are now farther back from the road, separated by vast stretches of dark lawn. She can barely see his face.

Of course, he will never own a house like this. These houses belong to pop stars and the Russian mob.

Even now, he is frowning and pausing at a crossroad, turning his head side to side. "I don't . . ." He wheels the car to the right.

It slows to a stop.

"Ooops, dead end," he says. He turns to face her.

They are on a gravel road, surrounded by black shapes of pines. His headlights cast the only light. She looks at the uneven outline of his ridged skull, at the dark shadow of his face, at where she thinks his mouth should be.

It's him or me, she thinks. Him or me. Him or me.

And I am willing.

She smothers him with her mouth.

She tongues the hollow beneath his Adam's apple.

She shoves her hand under his sweater and pinches his nipples.

She pushes back his head with both hands, to expose his neck, and bites.

Only when his hands begin to dig into her shoulders does she stop. He has made an X with his arms in front of his chest, palms facing outward, pushing her away.

She grabs at his groin, but he swats away her hand and says, "I thought you were shy."

His voice is querulous and accusing, his breathing uneven. "I watched you at the club. You barely moved your hands or body when you spoke. You took up as little space as possible. Very shy people do that . . ."

"You profiled me?"

" . . . or liars."

The adrenalin that rushed through her body a few minutes ago seems to have pooled in her stomach, leaving her legs and arms numb. She feels tired. No, exhausted. The heft of her disappointment and humiliation, surely, will capsize the car.

"I have no idea how we're going to get back," he says, and she turns towards the windshield. The yellow arm of a barrier gate extends across the road in front of them.

They are both lost. Lost in this suburb of designer homes. A dream of a dream she had when she was much younger.

"I won't hurt you," she says. She remains still. She makes no sudden movements.

"Liar," he whispers.

ANDREW BODEN

CONFLUENCE OF SPOORS

The hunter followed the blood down from the North Shore Mountains into Vancouver. This was the third day he'd tracked the buck his father wounded but couldn't kill, because a fall broke the old man's femur. The hunter had never known a buck to bleed this much and go on. It should have bedded down and died two days ago, but here were drops of its blood on the white shoulder line of the Upper Levels Highway and, a mile on, a tuft of tawny hair caught on a chain-link fence. He crossed the Lions Gate Bridge at dusk and followed the blood trail east past Coal Harbour, down Cordova Street into the lower East Side. Twice his .30-06 leapt to his shoulder, but the crosshairs fell on the ghosts of old kills and he cursed his exhaustion, his hunger. His image of the wounded buck, blood staining its white belly, blood trickling down its pink-white thighs, blood loss lowering its head inch by inch, pushed him past the broken women who all smiled and asked if he wanted a date. He came to Powell and Raymur and the blood trail went north and east.

He peered both ways through his scope: at the desolate

parking lot of the sugar refinery; at the dark road east. "Where are you?" he hissed. He wanted to shoot off a couple of rounds, fucking have done with it. It had drizzled for two days and his wet mackinaw and wool shirt made him itch with cold. Hunger was making him see double, he concluded, but neither blood trail, north or east, vanished after he downed a handful of bread crumbs from his pocket.

"Where is she?"

The hunter thought he imagined the voice, as he had imagined the branching bloody trails, but there was a woman now in a navy pea jacket beside him. She swept the eastern road, back and forth, with binoculars.

"*He*," he said. "A muley buck. Six point."

"*She*," the woman said. "My sister. That's her stroll two blocks back. She called last night and said she was in trouble. I called the cops, but . . ."

The hunter knelt down and touched both sets of tracks with his index fingers and brought them to his nose. Copper, gasoline, ocean rot – he couldn't tell which was human, which was deer. The buck would die, curl up behind a dumpster, get plucked to bone by crows and rats and the carcass buried in a Cache Creek landfill. No way to die, not a six-point beauty. As for the woman's sister, he pictured a similar end for her. No way to die? He didn't know anything of her beauty, inner or outer, enough to say.

"I'll go a little ways in both directions," he said. "Look for signs. Maybe a hoofprint, maybe dung or hair. It's a full moon – sometimes his shadow leaves impressions."

"Can you see the impressions a person's shadow leaves behind?"

"If the light is right."

"Is the light right?"

The ghosts the hunter's scope showed him half an hour ago, the ghosts of those old kills; he couldn't remember if they were all animals. And whose old kills? Who left them there on an urban street? It was his hunger thinking again. "For deer the light is right."

"Help me find her."

The hunter went a little way in both directions: north up the railway tracks and east along the road, but there was no sign of the buck.

"If your sister is bleeding like this buck is bleeding, then she hasn't got long."

The woman looked towards the parallel rows of lights on Grouse Mountain. They seemed to define a wide, curving road that went deep into the night sky.

"I can only follow one path," the hunter said. "Maybe your sister is there, maybe not."

The hunter went east, a few paces in front of the woman, towards Franklin Street. The low buildings closed around him and the further he went down the grubby road, the uneasier he grew. There were signs everywhere. A red condom hung from a blackberry vine. A hypodermic stuck up from the belly of a rag doll. A white ankle boot with a stiletto heel disappeared behind the passenger door of a black Escalade. In the lot of a burnt-down house, the grass was flattened as if animals had bedded down there. "What colour was your sister's hair?" the hunter asked. He passed the woman three blonde hairs he'd found on a pile of blankets and garbage.

"Bleached blonde. Brown before – I won't cry, you know.

Our lives divided. Val went one way and I went the other. Sometimes she called every day, sometimes weeks passed. Her last call was the first in two months."

The hunter split his last digestive biscuit in half and gave a piece to the woman. It was the only food he'd eaten in a day.

The black Escalade they'd seen earlier ejected a teenage girl in a pink fur coat and then her ankle boot. She limped down the street and wiped the blood from her nose with the sleeve of her coat.

"Are there men like this where you come from?" the woman asked.

"I didn't think so," the hunter said. "Not until tonight. You follow a trail – a broken branch, a footprint, some leavings – and you're surprised when it leads back to yourself."

"Did you do something like that? Even once?"

"I meant there were signs. Left after my thoughts. I don't go where they go."

The hunter and the woman followed the bloody trail south and then west, until grey dawn. Blood spatters wound up and down the streets, daubed a curb on Triumph and streaked a yellow cement barrier near Pandora. The woman found a black pump split at the heel, in the parking lot behind the Waldorf Pub. "It's Val's," she said. "Size seven."

They heard sirens from the southwest.

"He can't be far," the hunter said.

"*She*," the woman said.

The woman led the hunter at a run. They crossed Hastings into Strathcona and ran after the sirens. The buck was close now, the hunter could feel it; his heart sped up, his hands turned cold. Those ghosts of those old kills, he didn't need his scope to see them now. They moved everywhere in the shadows; each overlaid another, limbs entwined with limbs, torsos entwined with torsos, innards with innards. He wouldn't call them human.

The air grew heavy with the scent of cherry blossoms. A police car with its lights flashing sped away up another street. A crowd of men and women were gathered in the middle of East Pender. Some of them held candles and they sang a song the hunter didn't recognize. The blood trail led right up to the crowd.

"Val!" the woman cried and ran towards them.

If the buck is there, the hunter thought, at least he isn't suffering anymore. If Val is there, at least she isn't suffering anymore. He could go home, back to the hospital to visit his father. Get warm again. Get off this path.

His rifle leapt to his shoulder. The buck's antlers pushed past the corner of a large brick building. The hunter began to exhale as he waited for the buck's head to appear.

The woman sobbed. "Val!"

The hunter exhaled all his breath. His finger squeezed the trigger.

There! The buck's head and neck came past the comer of the building, but it was twisted at an impossible angle as if broken and wrenched too far to the right. The beast was moving, floating as if it were on its side, asleep on the arms of a strong wind. But it didn't move under the wind's power or even its own. The buck lay splayed across the front of the black Escalade, tied down with yellow rope. Its body steamed in the cold night; its blood cooked on the left headlight.

"Val! Val, come back!"

The crowd pressed in around the hunter. The ghosts of those old kills pressed in around the hunter. The crowd implored him with tears and sobs. Where they'd held their vigil, where the tracks he and the woman followed ended, there was a tangle of bloodied trails. Blood led off in every direction up the street – into desolate buildings, into the yards of houses. Some of it stopped where parked cars had been, some of it led to dumpsters.

He thought for a long time about which trail to follow. He feared they all led back to him. He feared what lay at the end of his thoughts.

LAURA BOUDREAU

THE DEAD DAD GAME

I liked the way Nate told the story. He was happy to reel it off, starting with the part where Genevieve, his first mother, collapsed on the kitchen floor with a blood clot in her lung. "It only took a second or two for her to die," he said, slowly lowering his hand in a side-to-side motion as though his mother had been a piece of windblown paper. "She probably didn't even feel it." Nate was a baby when it happened, and he had almost cried himself to death by the time the landlord unlocked the apartment door. His father – our father – lived with my mother by then. The day Genevieve died, my mother was busy giving birth. "But don't feel bad, Elaine," Nate said to me. "You almost died, too. You were early."

It seemed obvious to us that Genevieve's death was a lot better than our father's. It was definitely faster and there were no hospitals or operations, and Genevieve didn't have to lose her hair or spend a lot of time throwing up into stainless-steel bowls. My mother agreed with us on principle, she said, catching our eyes in the rearview mirror, but either way it wasn't appropriate to make a sport out of it. "Death isn't a contest, you know. Everyone gets the same prize." She lifted one hand from the steering wheel to make the point as we drove through the cemetery gates. Genevieve and our father were in different sections, but my mother said it was still very convenient for visiting, even if the traffic in this part of the city was hell.

We remembered our father a little, Nate more than me because he was older. Our mother encouraged us to ask all the questions we wanted, which helped us make up a few more memories. No topic was off-limits when it came to our dead parents. My mother didn't want us to grow up feeling guilty or resentful about things we didn't understand. "Fear is the source of all disease," she said as she made our kale breakfast shakes. She wasn't sure what our father had been afraid of, and we knew the theory didn't apply as well to Genevieve, but Nate and I bought into it anyway. We had a lot of questions.

"Did he walk with a cane?" Nate asked.

"Yes," our mother said, scraping the clogged blades of the Cuisinart with a wooden spoon. "He tried, anyway. He didn't want a ramp out front. We'd already spent a lot of money on the landscaping."

"What colour were his glasses?"

"He didn't wear glasses, Nate. You know that."

"And what about his eyelashes?" I asked. I felt left out because I mostly remembered him as a shadow that smelled like Vicks VapoRub. "Did they fall out in clumps?" Nate said that our father had pink eye a lot and sometimes wore sunglasses to watch television.

"This blender."

The more questions we asked, the more my mother's face went strange. The bones in her jaw looked like they had softened and stretched. It was uncomfortable to watch her when she talked like that. I felt like we were scaring her, which was the worst thing you could do to a person, in my book. Nate was going on about radiation therapy and its scientific connections to superpowers, and my mother's face kept shifting, like I was looking at her underwater. She rested the spoon on the stove-top and rolled up the sleeve of her dressy black sweater to pick at the blades, and Nate kept firing question after question: Was our dad ever a Cub Scout? Did he drink kale shakes? Which one of the three of us did he love most?

Nate had once told me that mothers, as much as you might love them, were all the same. He said that if anything happened to my mother, another lady would adopt the two of us, maybe one of our aunts in Philadelphia or Newark. Women loved babies most, he said, but we were still little enough to be okay. "It's fathers who are the tough ones. Much harder to come by."

Nate was living proof. I heard the way my mother tucked him into the bunk above me, telling him to close his eyes, sleepy bird, and dream of flying over all the green places on the Earth, but he still had to play the Father-Son Scout Baseball Tournament with Mr. Crisander. Mr. Crisander did up all the buttons on his polo shirts and parted his hair down the middle. At Halloween he gave out toothbrushes. He said Nate could call him Captain as a kind of nickname, but Nate stuck to Mr. Crisander. Mr. Crisander lived alone next door with his pot-bellied pig, Mickey, who had been starved by her previous owners to make her small. It had worked, to a point.

Now she was about the size of our Aunt Jennifer's fat beagle, and she came if Mr. Crisander called her, but Mickey was a lot heavier than a dog and had stumpy legs. She couldn't catch a Frisbee to save her life. She also had a bad skin disease. Her raw, scaly hide showed through her black and white bristles. Sometimes she scratched against the stone pillar near the bottom of our driveway and her back oozed. Still, none of our friends could say they knew a pet pig, and she seemed to like us. Nate and I felt like we had to pet Mickey if we saw her.

"I found Mick through the SPCA," Mr. Crisander said as Mickey plowed her snout into our limp fingers. "People buy them and think they'll stay piglets forever." Mickey seemed like a good enough pig, but it made us uneasy that she rubbed against our legs, shimmying and squealing. She also had a bad habit of rooting in my mother's garden. "Leave that thing for long enough," my mother had said, throwing out what was left of her tulips, "and it'll dig up the dead." It didn't help Mickey's case that our mother told us to wash our hands after we touched her. It made us think certain things about Mickey, and about Mr. Crisander. Nate had recently mentioned he didn't want to go to Scouts anymore, and my mother said she had been thinking the same thing. "I mean, a father-son baseball game? What are we, Republicans?" Nate went to Science Club now, and he was collecting cans to save money for his own microscope.

My mother didn't mind that Nate kept a picture of Genevieve taped to the ceiling above his pillow. Genevieve had a big pink flower behind one ear and her nose was sunburned. He didn't really miss her, he said, because how could you miss someone you didn't have space for? I felt like I knew what he meant. This was why we didn't have questions about Genevieve, why her death sounded like a grocery list of events and why we never played the game with her. It was our father who was the hole in our lives.

"Did he die in the morning or at night?"

"Morning."

"How did you know he was dead?"

"He stopped breathing."

"Did his heart stop beating, too?"

"After a minute, yes."

"What happened then?"

My mother's face was sliding out from under her skin. She whacked at the blades with the spoon.

"Fucking blender," she said.

She flung the spoon across the counter and it smashed into Nate's shake. We jumped as the glass hit the tiles and the spoon clattered under the dining room table. Gobs of kale splattered onto Nate's suit pants as the glass broke apart with a barely audible click. The three of us looked at the mess on the floor. I started to cry.

My mother quickly picked up the biggest pieces of glass, the clink of them in her hand like a stunted wind chime. "He was dead, Nate. Nothing happened then." She wrapped the shards in a sheet of newspaper and threw the package in the garbage. "Don't cry about the glass, Elaine. If we were Buddhists, we'd already think of it as broken. Now go put your shoes on and wait for me in the car. And don't pet Mickey if she's in the driveway."

The drive was quiet, just the sound of Stevie Wonder from the tape deck. When we got close, our mother sang along softly. Nate and I didn't look at each other. Instead we watched the people on the sidewalk and tried to guess their names. Nate said the woman with the puppy in her bike basket was a Shirley, but I thought she was a Tory. We agreed that the man with the bundle buggy full of wine bottles was a George. We couldn't quite decide on the woman with the fabric shopping bags and bunches of sunflowers. A Rebecca, we thought, or maybe a Donna.

"A Genevieve," my mother said. "You can always tell a Genevieve. Nate, do you feel like telling Elaine the story?" We knew this was her way of asking us to forgive her, which we did right away. It was just a glass.

"She had a blood clot in her lung, which is also called a thrombus," Nate started, and the story went from there.

The cemetery roadways were narrow and our mother drove slowly in case a car came from the other way, which it almost never did. The grass was neatly mowed. Any fresh mounds of dirt were covered with strips of bright green sod, making it look like the newer graves had more life in them. Some of the headstones, usually the ones with carvings of angels or inset pictures of Jesus, even pictures of the person who died, had lots of flowers around them. There were carnations in sturdy vases and votive candles everywhere. Our mother told us that people paid extra to have the cemetery staff come and leave those things once a month, once a week, if you really wanted to, but she said it didn't matter how many flowers there were, it was the love you left that was important. "Cemetery workers are paid to care," she shrugged. "Dead people may be dead, but they can still tell the difference. Not that we're judging."

We parked the car and Nate got the beach towel out of the trunk. The ground was a little soft and our mother's high heels sunk into the grass, kicking up lopsided cones of dirt as we headed over to our father's grave. She started walking on the balls of her feet, knees bent. "God," she said, "I feel like a praying mantis." She took off her shoes and hooked one finger into each heel, the toes dangling.

"Praying mantises eat each other when they mate," Nate said.

"Actually, that's not true." My mother tapped the toes of her shoes together. "They only do that in laboratories when people are watching."

"But we saw them do it in the wild, on TV," I said.

"Well, somebody had to be holding the camera, don't you think?"

I helped Nate spread the beach towel lengthwise over our father's grave. It was yellow and it had a hot pink flamingo wearing pineapple-shaped sunglasses. Our mother bought it on sale. She said that most people probably found it a bit loud, even for the beach, but that's what the graveyard needed, wasn't it? A little colour.

"How would you like to live with only grey furniture?" she asked us, pointing at the gravestones. But it didn't really matter. All the towel had to do was keep our graveyard clothes clean.

Our father's name was carved into a large polished piece of granite, and then below that it said, "Son, Husband, Father, Caregiver." When Nate was younger, he had asked our mother if our father worked in schools or office buildings.

"That's a caretaker, Nate. A janitor. Your father was a doctor."

"So why couldn't he make himself better?"

"Why can't pigs fly?"

"They're mammals."

"So was your dad."

When Nate and I were done smoothing out the towel, my mother laid out a framed picture of us as a family, me in my mother's arms and Nate teetering on one tiny running shoe with his fists around my father's fingers. Beside that she stacked some oatmeal chocolate chip cookies. She thought the game worked better if we didn't have low blood sugar. She brushed the dirt off the bottoms of her bare feet and tied her hair back with an elastic band. "Okay, who wants to go first this time?"

The game wasn't the kind that Nate and I played with our friends. The kids we hung out with were mostly into four square and dodgeball and a kind of football that we made up and called Astronaut. Those games had a winner and rules, teams, but the Dead Dad Game didn't have any of that. All we did was lie very still on the beach towel and listen, and to make our mother happy we sometimes made things up when she asked us, "What do you hear?" In a lot of ways it wasn't a game at all, but there was nothing else to call it. My mother said it was a game. It was just something we did.

"Nate, why don't you go?" My mother passed him a cookie. "Take your shoes off before you get on the towel."

Nate undid the laces of his stiff black shoes and lined them up beside my mother's high heels. He sat down and took a few deep breaths. My mother and I moved closer, perching on the edge of the towel to save our skirts, and Nate closed his eyes. My mother held out her hand to me and then we each took one of Nate's hands in ours, closing the circle. He wriggled in his suit.

"Wouldn't it be better if we just wore regular clothes?" I asked.

"It's more respectful this way." My mother squeezed our hands. "And people won't bug us as much if it looks like we came from a church. Now let's be quiet so Nate can listen."

My mother said that when bodies broke down and turned into grass and soil, there were vibrations. That's all that talking was, vibrations, so being dead didn't mean that you stopped talking, even if it wasn't in the same language. Nate had asked his science club teacher what she thought about that, and she said she hadn't heard the theory before, but there were a lot of things that still needed to be discovered in the world. That was the point of the club. Nate was convinced, or said he was.

"I hear," he paused, "I hear humming."

"That makes sense," my mother said slowly, but I didn't think it made sense at all. Why would our dad's body be humming? Was there that much to hum about when you were dead? Maybe he was just happy to see us, I thought. That was possible. Or maybe Nate was faking. That was possible, too. I faked.

"Can I have a cookie?" I asked.

"In a minute, Elaine," my mother said. "What else do you hear?"

The three of us closed our eyes and listened hard. I saw our father's vibrations crawling up like earthworms, tickling Nate's back with secret messages about how much he missed us, about the things that had made him afraid and sick. Our mother said that visualization was an important part of the game, and she always seemed to hear things, grunts or mumbles. I just needed to visualize harder, and then I would hear it too. Faking wasn't lying, it was practicing. Nate was about to say something else, but we heard a car door slam. We dropped our hands and opened our eyes.

It was the red cemetery maintenance truck. Two guys in matching windbreakers and baseball hats were fishing around in the flatbed. One of them grabbed a rake, and the other one hugged a giant bag of garden fertilizer.

"Shit," my mother said, and the game was over.

Nate balled up the towel and shoved it under his arm. He squashed his feet into his shoes, breaking down the backs. My mother shook out her hair. I packed the picture and cookies into her purse. My mother waved to the men as she hustled us to the car, and the one man raised his rake to us while the other one slit the fertilizer bag with a packing knife. We didn't play the game while other people watched. It didn't work that way, and there had been problems before. My mother told us that a lot of people have pretty un-evolved ideas about things. She had written letters to the cemetery's managing director about the behaviour of his employees.

"Let's not worry about it too much," she said, pushing play on the stereo. "It's not like your dad won't be here next Sunday. Seat belts." We drove past Genevieve's grave on the way out. Nate waved.

We were almost home before I asked about the humming. My mother said that the whole universe hummed, that if we heard everybody's heartbeats, all at once, it would sound like the buzzing of a beehive. "We're all connected," she said.

"But what if you don't have a heartbeat?" I asked. "What about all the dead people?"

"I watched a show about bees," Nate said. "If you put a box of them in the freezer, they clump around the queen to keep her warm. After a few hours, you have this pile of dead bees."

"Were they killer bees?" my mother said. "Good hygiene is as important as a clear conscience."

My mother spun the steering wheel with the flat of one hand and leaned over to pop out the Stevie Wonder tape as we turned into our driveway. Nate was already unbuckling his seatbelt when my mother – "Oh shit," she said – swerved and jammed the brakes. The car lurched, hard, and Nate slammed into the back of the passenger seat. There was the hollow thud of metal hitting something softer than itself, and then right away a kind of shriek that at first I thought was Nate, and then I thought was my mother, my mother who wasn't like any other mother, no matter what Nate said, but then the shriek came again, from outside the car, again and again, until it died away and became softer, deeper, more like a humming.

"Oh shit," my mother said again. She took the keys out of the ignition. We got out of the car.

It wasn't actually a hum at all, once we heard it better. It was more of a phlegmy growl, a snuffling, and it was so steady that it didn't seem to matter if Mickey was breathing in or breathing out, and for a second I didn't think she was doing either. Her back legs were bent towards her tail and her feet were bleeding. Part of one leg was skinned. The muscle was pink and twitchy and looked like the kind of thing my mother refused to buy in chain grocery stores. Our front bumper was fine, but there was a strip of skin hanging underneath the car.

"Nate, get the toboggan," my mother said calmly, bending down and stroking Mickey's head with two fingers. But Nate stood there, fiddling with the car door handle, staring at Mickey as she groaned and licked my mother's wrist. "Nate." He slammed the door and took off for the garage. "Elaine, get the towel out of the trunk."

Nate ran with the toboggan scraping behind him on the asphalt. We lined it up beside Mickey and I laid the towel out over its wooden slats. My mother grabbed Mickey around the chest and hauled her up, letting her legs hang. "Jesus," she said, doing a power squat. Mickey shook as my mother lowered her onto the toboggan. Mickey's tongue hung out of her mouth. She was shivering and panting. I wrapped her in the towel and her legs felt like bags of loose marbles. The blood leaked through the pink flamingo and turned it orange.

My mother dragged the toboggan to Mr. Crisander's and Nate and I walked beside, each of us with a steadying hand on Mickey to make sure she didn't fall off. Mickey made squeaking noises when we tried to tilt the toboggan up the steps, and we decided that was a bad idea. My mother went up on the porch to ring the doorbell and I sat beside Mickey, keeping her company and whispering in her ear that she was a good girl, such a good girl, while she pawed at my arm with one of her front hooves. Nate got a stick and went back to the car. He started poking gently at the swinging skin. My mother rang the doorbell again and we waited. Then she knocked.

"If he's not home," she said, "we're going to have to take care of this ourselves." She watched me stroke gently under Mickey's chin with one finger. "Look at her."

I patted Mickey, pressing on her chest softly until I felt the fluttering of her heart and she let out a little grunt. This was taking care of her, I thought, wrapping her in a beach towel and keeping her warm so she might stop shivering.

"Elaine."

I was never going to let her go.

Mr. Crisander opened the door with an apron on and a checkered dish towel over one shoulder. His house smelled like burnt sugar. He patted his belly happily when he saw my mother.

"Natalie, I was ju–" His eyes flicked down to me and Mickey and he stopped. His mouth kept moving but I didn't understand the words that came out. He held his arms out and Mickey snuffled, closing her eyes. The towel was soaked. The words from Mr. Crisander turned into something that sounded like, "Mickey Mick-Mick, Mickey Mick-Mick." He said it over and over as he drifted down the stairs with his arms out to her, like I was invisible and it was just Mickey he saw, begging for him to hold onto her before she disappeared like a dream he didn't remember. I draped one arm over Mickey and hugged her close.

"Elaine," my mother said again, more sharply. Mr. Crisander's arms kept gliding towards me, saying, "Mickey, Mick-Mick," until I felt Mickey shift under me. She made a noise that was almost a honk as Mr. Crisander picked her up. He moved effortlessly, like Mickey weighed nothing at all. He climbed the stairs and went inside without saying anything to us.

"John," my mother started, "if there's something –" but the door was already closed. Nate crouched by the tire. My cemetery blouse had pig blood on it, and my mother held her arms out in front of her, her wrists limp.

"Let's go wash our hands," she said.

It was a surprise to all of us that Mickey didn't die. She was back a few days later, lying in the bay window of Mr. Crisander's living room on a new and very plush white bed. Her back end was wrapped in gauze and an adult diaper with a hole cut out for her tail. Mr. Crisander changed her diaper every few hours, and it must have hurt her for him to do it; as soon as he started to unfasten the sticky tabs at the sides, Mickey's mouth opened and closed and we knew she was crying. My mother told us that she heard Mr. Crisander had taken a leave of absence from his job at the Veterans' Hospital. She tried phoning him, but he hung up as soon as she said, "John, it's Natalie." Nate and I left cards on the front porch, addressed to Mickey, but we saw them unopened in the recycling bin on garbage day. Mr. Crisander fed Mickey with a dinner spoon out of a large bowl and gave her water with an eyedropper. He did that for weeks, but Mickey's legs didn't seem to get any better.

On weekends Nate and I sat on the sidewalk outside Mr. Crisander's house and watched Mickey blink at us erratically. Sometimes we blinked back. Mickey didn't seem all that bad, we said. My mother agreed. "Some of the patchier parts of her skin look better," she noticed when she came to get us for dinner. Mr. Crisander ignored us, but he talked to Mickey a lot. Sometimes he turned her bed around so she was able to see the television while he watched old westerns. He even hung a cat toy from the ceiling for her, and Mickey batted it around and looked happy.

It was July before Mr. Crisander let us apologize. We were playing outside his house in our cemetery clothes. The sidewalk was cool, even though the sun was starting to steam the dew off the brown grass. It was getting hot and soon it would be scorching. Our mother was going to stripe our noses with neon green zinc, no matter what we had to say about it. If we didn't want skin cancer, she said, we were just going to have to put up with looking like idiots once in a while.

Nate leaned back on his elbows and watched Mickey blink. I drew pictures of pigs with sidewalk chalk. I made dozens of Mickeys, some with legs and some without, but all of them with big smiles on their faces and little noise lines coming off of them like they were alarm clocks. I was working on a very large and purple Mickey when Nate tapped my arm with his foot.

"Elaine," he said. "He's looking."

Mr. Crisander stood in the window and crossed his arms. He was wearing a bathrobe, and he had Mickey's bowl in one of his hands. Mickey was stretching her leg out at the food, but Mr. Crisander just kept staring at us. We had been waiting for this. We were sorry. My mother said that acceptance was the last stage of grief and we couldn't rush Mr. Crisander. We could only make offerings to him, and to Mickey. "Sidewalk chalk is good," she said. "If he's only made it as far as the anger stage and he flips out, I can just stretch the garden hose over. Sometimes guys like him flip out."

Nate and I stood up and waved to Mr. Crisander. He didn't wave back. Nate shouted, "Our thoughts are with you and Mickey at this difficult time." I pointed to the Mickeys on the sidewalk, their smiling faces like blue and green and purple suns, glowing, and their sound lines speaking to me: Hi, Elaine. I see you.

Mr. Crisander drew the curtains.

"Anger stage," Nate said.

I drew a few more chalk pigs and Nate watched the Mickey-shaped shadow behind the sheers. We were hopeful.

Mr. Crisander came out onto the porch. He had changed into bright blue jeans and a white T-shirt with sleeves that went past his elbows. He started for the sidewalk. Nate buttoned his suit jacket and I brushed the chalk off my hands. Mr. Crisander stood on his lawn and studied the upside-down chalk Mickeys.

"Do you know where pigs like Mickey come from?" he asked.

We didn't.

"Vietnam," he said. His eyes paused on the giant purple Mickey. "My son lives there."

"You have a son?" Nate was surprised. Mr. Crisander was terrible at baseball. "What's he doing in Vietnam?"

"Does Mickey ever get homesick?" I asked.

"Let's have some Kool-Aid," Mr. Crisander said. "Mickey misses you two."

We had never been inside Mr. Crisander's house before. My mother drove us to and from the baseball games and sat in the stands and read a magazine. She said that the baseball diamond was one thing but a person's house was another. If Mr. Crisander ever invited us in, we were supposed to check with her first. "All I'm saying is, better safe than on Geraldo," she said. But Mr. Crisander had never asked before and he might not ask again. Nate and I wanted to see Mickey. We followed him up the front walk.

His house was the same as ours – the living room was to the left of the front door, and on the other side there were twisty stairs to the basement, and down the middle, a hallway that led to the kitchen – but Mr. Crisander's house seemed bigger because it was so empty. In our living room we had a sofa that turned into a bed, a loveseat, a bookshelf, and a big coffee table that my mother buffed with Pledge before my aunts came over. Mr. Crisander only had a rabbit ear TV and a VCR, and and olive green wingback chair that was rubbed down to beige on one side. Mickey blinked at us from her bed in the window seat.

"Look who's here, Mickey," Mr. Crisander said loudly. We stood in the alcove and waved. Mickey blinked back.

"She's doing a lot better," Mr. Crisander said more softly to us. "But the vet says she's a little heavy from the lack of exercise. I'm thinking of making her a wheelchair she can power with her front legs."

Mickey's front legs looked like spindly little toothpicks that had been jammed into her giant watermelon body, but we didn't say anything.

"We'll be in the kitchen if you need us, Mickey," Mr. Crisander shouted. "Her hearing's going," he said as we walked down the hallway.

Mr. Crisander dumped two packets of Kool-Aid powder into a big blue pitcher, but he filled it to the brim without even measuring and he didn't stir for long enough. The Kool-Aid tasted like water but looked like pale blood.

"Would you like to see Mickey's room?" he asked.

"Mickey has her own room?" I couldn't believe it. Mickey was the luckiest pig in the world.

"We have bunk beds," Nate said as Mr. Crisander took us back down the hall.

"Well, pigs aren't very good with ladders," he said.

Mickey's room was painted light purple. She had a wooden scratching post drilled into the floor and a large rope with big knots that was probably a toy. There was a giant teddy bear losing his stuffing from a hole in his face, and a beanbag chair with a Mickey-sized depression still in the middle of it. In the corner of the room there was a large dog house in the shape of an igloo. Inside it we saw a fluffy pink comforter. Mickey also had a radio. It was set high on a wooden shelf near the top of the window, and it was tuned to the same station my mother liked.

"What do you think?"

Next to the radio was a small picture in a gold frame. The photo was blurry and old, the corners of it yellow and blotchy. It was even harder to see because it was up so high, but we could tell it was of a woman with long dark hair and tiny eyes. She wore a funny-looking pointed hat that cast a big shadow over her face, but I still saw that she had a hand over her mouth. She might have been smiling.

"Is that your wife?" Nate pointed. Suddenly it seemed possible that someone like Mr. Crisander might have a wife.

"No," Mr. Crisander said, "she's not."

Nate and I finished our drinks. "Thanks for the Kool-Aid. It was really good," I lied.

Mr. Crisander told us we were welcome any time we liked. Any friend of Mickey's was a friend of his, and bygones were bygones.

"Maybe on Friday night you guys can come over and watch a movie," he said as we made our way to the front door. "Give your mom a break. I'll make popcorn."

Maybe, we said, but right now we had to go. It was Sunday and we were already late.

DEVON CODE

UNCLE OSCAR

The first time Oscar asked to stay with them, Leo's mother said, "I don't want no dope fiend hanging around my son." But he showed up again two weeks later, the night after Leo's thirteenth birthday. He walked right in the front door and stood in the kitchen with his seven-string Ibanez electric guitar slung over his shoulder. He had nothing else with him at all, not even a jacket. He said he needed a loan, or else he needed somewhere to stay where no one could find him. He said he was going to stay clean for sure this time, and that he owed some guy a lot of money.

Leo's mother put her fork down on her plate. She held her hand up to her forehead, which was creased, and she closed her eyes, like she was in pain. She suddenly looked old to Leo, like she was a very old woman instead of just a mom. When she opened her eyes a moment later, she looked angry and sad at the same time. She held on to the kitchen table with both hands then, tightly. She stared at Leo the whole time, as if she was really talking to him and not his uncle. She said that she was a hairdresser with a kid to support and that she didn't have money to loan anybody, but that Oscar could stay in the basement for a while if he needed to. She said she didn't trust him, after the way he'd left before, and that she probably never would. He'd be locked in, she explained, because the only way to get out was through the kitchen and she didn't want him going around upstairs when she wasn't home. She said he could come upstairs in the evenings and have dinner with them, and that she'd keep some food for him in the mini-fridge downstairs, and buy his smokes, so long as he paid her back when he got clean.

"Any sign of coke," she said, "or any of that shit and you're out. And you can't smoke around Leo."

"No problem," said Oscar. "I can handle that." Then he stood his guitar against the fridge and sat down next to Leo on the cat-hair covered chair where Mr. Tibbs would sit when no one else was in the room. Uncle Oscar's eyes were red and he hadn't shaved in a while. His hands shook as he ate and he kept dropping goulash on his Sepultura T-shirt. He hardly ate anything at all, even though it looked like it had been a while since he'd had a meal. He gave off a sweet smell like brown bananas, and Leo didn't eat very much either. As soon as Uncle Oscar finished, he picked up his guitar and went downstairs.

"What about Mr. Tibbs?" Leo asked his mom. "How's he going to use the bathroom?"

"We'll have to bring the kitty litter upstairs for a while."

"How's Uncle Oscar supposed to use the bathroom?"

"There's the laundry sink. He can use that," his mother said. Then she told Leo that before he was allowed to play croquet he had to go upstairs and get a spare set of sheets and bring them down to his uncle, and then bring the kitty litter up to the kitchen.

"But what if there's a fire?" said Leo. "And I'm at school and you're at work? How will Uncle Oscar get out?"

"He can climb out through the basement window any time he wants," she said. "He's not really trapped down there."

"Oh," said Leo.

When Leo went downstairs his uncle was slouched on the couch with his feet on an upside-down milk crate. He was watching *Wheel of Fortune* on the old TV set and smoking a cigarette. He'd taken off his workboots and left them beside the milk crate, their tops flopped over. His wool socks were worn through at the heel. As soon as he saw Leo, he stubbed his cigarette out in an empty flower pot. "Thanks, kiddo," he said.

Leo put the sheets down beside him and tried not to cough. "How long you going to stay?" he said.

"Not long."

Leo went over to get the kitty litter and when he passed the laundry sink it smelled like barf. He looked inside and the stainless steel was clean and wet.

"Where's your Harley?" he asked.

"Sold it."

"What'd you get for it?"

"A grand."

"Is that more than the money you owe?"

"No."

Leo thought about that for a moment. He wondered how much coke someone would have to do in order to owe someone that much money and decided it would have to be a lot. In the drawer of Leo's bedside table there were two brand new twenty dollar bills that his mother had just given him for his birthday. Like he was just trying to make conversation, he said, "How much does coke usually cost?" But his uncle kept watching *Wheel of Fortune* like he hadn't heard the question.

Leo looked at the tiny window on the far wall, just below the ceiling. Beneath the window was a wheelbarrow full of gardening tools that his mother hadn't used in years. He thought that if he turned the wheelbarrow over and stood on it, he could reach the window and squeeze through. He thought his uncle probably could fit through too, but he wasn't sure.

When Leo came back upstairs his mother was washing the supper dishes, her back turned to him.

"Close the door," she said. "Lock the deadbolt." There was a plate with three peanut butter cookies on the kitchen table and Leo sat down. His mother told him she didn't want him spending any more time with his uncle than he had to. She told Leo they had to be extra careful to keep the front door locked from now on, and that he had to keep the basement door locked whenever they weren't home. Then she rinsed the dish soap off her hands and dried them with a tea towel. She turned from the sink to face Leo, placed a hand on each of his shoulders, and looked him in the eye.

"Your uncle," she said, "cannot be trusted. But I know I can trust you. Promise me you won't tell anyone he's staying here."

"No problem," Leo said. "I can handle that."

Leo managed to not tell anyone about Uncle Oscar for a whole week. But then on Monday after school he told his friend Francesco that his uncle had a seven-string Ibanez electric guitar, and that he used to have a custom Harley, but that he didn't have his bike anymore because he was a dope fiend and was living in the basement. He said he stayed down there all day, watching TV and smoking and pissing in the laundry sink, and that he was strung out when he first came to stay with them, but now he seemed like he was clean. He told Francesco that he didn't like having another man around the house, and that he hated the kitty litter stink in the kitchen. Then Francesco looked at him like he wasn't listening, so Leo said, "You want to play croquet with me in the parkette right now? I've got money so we can go to the store after."

"Fuck that shit," said Francesco. "I got a game in Mississauga." Francesco was the sweeper for the Saint Erbin Academy boys' soccer team. He also knew how to play four songs on the guitar and he had a girlfriend named Isabel, who wasn't bad looking.

"Probably be rained out," said Leo.

"So how you gonna play croquet?"

"See you tomorrow," said Leo. Then he left and went and got on the southbound bus. The bus was crowded with kids in Saint Erbin uniforms: grey polyester old-man pants and black running shoes. Most of them wore sweatshirts to cover up their maroon Saint Erbin golf shirts, even though it was too humid for long sleeves. The bus stank of deodorant and Leo found it hard to breathe. He took his puffer from his front pocket and inhaled and thought about what he hadn't told Francesco. On Saturday afternoon Leo's mother had told him to bring two tuna sandwiches down to the basement. When he'd opened the door, Mr. Tibbs ran down ahead of him and then Leo came down and found his uncle on the couch with his fly open, pumping his dick in his hand. His uncle put it away and started to do up his fly and Leo'd said, "Sorry," because he didn't know what else to say. "Don't worry about it," his uncle said and then took the sandwiches from him like it wasn't a big deal. Leo went upstairs to his room and punched his mattress three times as hard as he could. Then he locked the door and pulled down his pants and held his own dick in his hand. He tried to think about Francesco's girlfriend, Isabel, but he couldn't do anything because he kept picturing his uncle trying to jerk off, so he went to play croquet in the backyard instead.

When Leo got off the bus and walked up to the corner just before his street, the Camaro ss was parked there like always, with Ramon behind the wheel. The Camaro ss was black with white racing stripes. It had twin air vents on the hood and silver rims and was low to the ground and reminded Leo of a snake. Ramon had flat cheeks with little scars on them and he wore a black Blue Jays ball cap with a gold sticker on its brim, and black wraparound sunglasses even though the sky was dark and grey. His seat was reclined and he was leaning back. Leo knew he was nineteen years old, because his mother used to babysit Ramon when he was seven and Leo was one. His mother would talk about Ramon sometimes, about when she would stay at home looking after the two of them, before Leo's father left and she took the job at DivaMax. Leo had been too young to remember, but he could tell by the way Ramon looked at him that he knew who he was. Francesco had told Leo that Ramon sold weed and coke. Instead of crossing the street like he usually did, Leo walked up to Ramon's window and said, "How much is it for some coke?"

Ramon looked at him for a second and then looked away

and Leo couldn't tell what kind of expression was on his face because his glasses hid his eyes.

"Get out of here," said Ramon. But Leo just stood there. Ramon looked at him again and his face scrunched up like he was laughing, but he didn't make any sound. Then he took his sunglasses off and started to polish the lenses on his T-shirt. Leo thought that Ramon looked friendlier without his sunglasses on, and he figured that was why he wore them all the time.

"How much are we talking about?" said Ramon.

"You know," said Leo. "Enough."

"Fifty," said Ramon.

Leo thought that might be a fair price, but he said, "That's too much. You're charging too much for that shit," so Ramon wouldn't think he actually wanted to buy some. Ramon put his sunglasses back on and smiled and raised his eyebrows, as if Leo had said something funny. Leo turned then, and kept walking home, and he thought he heard Ramon say something about his mom, but he didn't turn around.

As soon as he got in the front door he could hear the TV on in the basement. He ran up to his room and took off his uniform and put on jeans and his New England Patriots T-shirt. He went to his bedside table and took out the two twenty dollar bills and slid them into the front pocket of his jeans. Then he picked up his croquet set and opened it up on the bed and looked at it for a minute. The wooden case was pitted and missing the yellow ball, but everything else was in good condition. He'd found the set in the basement last summer, looked up the rules in the *World Book Encyclopaedia*, and taught himself to play. He'd asked his mother where the set came from and she said his father must have gotten it somewhere, but that she couldn't remember him ever playing. Leo thought his father had probably played croquet a lot, and that his mother had just forgotten. He almost always played croquet by himself, but he knew it was more fun playing against someone else, even if they weren't very good. One time he'd played against Francesco in the backyard, and another time against his mom, and he'd beat them both pretty easily. He decided he'd ask his uncle to play a game in the backyard, even though he knew what he would say. He brought the croquet set downstairs and set it by the fridge, poured himself a glass of chocolate milk, and got four peanut butter cookies out of the bag in the cupboard. He unlocked the deadbolt on the basement door and stood at the top of the stairs and called out, "Uncle Oscar, it's me Leo."

"Leo," said his uncle, "come on down, my man." Mr. Tibbs flitted past Leo as soon as he started down the stairs. His uncle was slouched on the couch, watching a soap opera, and Mr. Tibbs ran over and sat on his stomach and curled up in a ball. Uncle Oscar had started shaving again and his hands had stopped shaking a while ago. He wore the same clothes he'd been wearing the day he showed up, except now over his Sepultura T-shirt he had on a ratty red and black button-down shirt that Leo's mom used to wear when she worked in the garden.

"You want a peanut butter cookie?" Leo asked.

"Too healthy."

"Is that a good show you're watching?"

"Nope."

"Uncle Oscar."

"Leo." Uncle Oscar picked up the remote from the cushion beside him and turned down the volume.

"How long were you a dope fiend for?"

Oscar laughed. His belly shook and Mr. Tibbs raised his head and glared at Leo and then set his head back down.

"On and off for three years."

Leo took a sip of chocolate milk. "What's going to happen if you don't pay back that money?"

Oscar closed his eyes and sank back in the couch.

"I'm going to pay it back."

Leo finished his cookies and set his milk glass down on the floor. He reached over and picked up his uncle's Ibanez guitar and held it in his lap. Uncle Oscar opened his eyes and looked at him for a second and then turned back towards the TV. Leo tried to play an E chord, but two of the strings were broken. He tried to write a song by plucking one string at a time, but he couldn't think of a tune that he liked. He thought his uncle might offer to show him how to play something, but Uncle Oscar just kept watching TV. Leo put the guitar back down and turned towards the screen. There was an old woman lying in a hospital bed and another woman in a fancy purple dress who was shouting at her, but the volume was turned down so low it was impossible to hear what they were saying.

"You going to move out of here?" asked Leo.

"Soon." Oscar nodded. "Very soon."

"Is it safe?"

"I can't stay down here forever."

"You want to play croquet in the parkette with me before you go?"

Oscar looked towards the basement window. "How'd you ever start playing a game like that?" he said.

"I have asthma."

"I know that, Leo."

"You remember when I was a baby and you were visiting and you'd just got your custom Harley? You put your helmet on me and held me up next to the bike in the driveway and Mom took a picture, or maybe it was my dad."

"I don't remember that."

"It's in the picture album upstairs. Are you going to get another bike when you get money again?"

Oscar stretched his legs and stroked Mr. Tibbs behind the ears and Mr. Tibbs flicked his tail. "I think maybe I'll get a car," said Oscar.

"What's faster, a motorbike or a car?"

"It depends on the bike and it depends on the car, but most of the time I'd say a bike's faster."

"Why would you get a car then?"

"Sometimes cars make more sense."

"Why?"

Uncle Oscar said nothing for a minute and watched the TV screen and stroked Mr. Tibbs's back. A man in a tuxedo had come into the hospital room, and he was trying to get the woman in the purple dress to leave. "Let's say you got some friends across town," said Uncle Oscar, finally, "and you want to get over there to play some croquet."

"In Mississauga," said Leo.

"Sure."

"I don't know anyone who lives in Mississauga."

"We're pretending."

"How many friends?"

"How many of those hammers you got?"

"What?"

"Croquet sticks."

"Mallets you mean?"

"How many?"

"Six."

"Let's say you got four friends over in Mississauga who want to play, and a buddy from North York who wants to play. That makes six of you. They got the perfect field in Mississauga. Nice and flat. Green grass."

"That's what the parkette is like," said Leo. "We can go there right now."

"They got some pretty girls over in Mississauga," Uncle Oscar continued, "who want to watch you play. How you gonna get you and your buddy over there, and all your gear without no car? What you need is a car."

"A Camaro ss."

"Good choice," said Uncle Oscar.

Leo imagined a field in Mississauga with wickets all set up and some girls there, who were cousins of Francesco's girl-friend, Isabel, and they were all wearing bikinis because it was so hot out. He imagined he was on the highway driving over there on a Harley and he had his favourite croquet mallet strapped to his back with a leather strap that he had custom-made. Francesco and the other guys there had bikes too, but they were Hondas. No one had a Camaro.

"How many girlfriends have you had?" asked Leo.

"Too many."

Leo wondered how many that might be. Then Uncle Oscar picked Mr. Tibbs up with both hands and set him down on the floor. He turned off the TV and said, "Leo, I need to take a crap. I'm going to go upstairs and take a crap. Then after we can go to that parkette and play some croquet before it rains, mano-a-mano. You cool with that?"

"I'm cool with that," said Leo, "if you want to." He tried to sound like he wasn't too excited, and then he waited before his uncle had gone all the way upstairs before he followed. As soon as Leo heard his uncle close the bathroom door, he realized he had to take a crap, too. Drinking chocolate milk always did that to him. He went up to the bathroom door, pressed his ear against it, and tried to hear what was going on inside. The fan was on and he thought he could hear his uncle singing or talking to himself, but he couldn't be sure. Leo stood there listening for a long time and eventually he wondered if his uncle was jerking off, or maybe getting high. He thought maybe there was a way to get high from shampoo or toothpaste that he didn't know about.

"Uncle Oscar," he yelled. "What are you doing in there?"

"What do you think?" his uncle yelled back.

"Are you going to be much longer?"

"Almost done."

"Do you want to see that picture before we go?"

"What picture?" said Uncle Oscar. Then he said, "Oh yeah. Sure."

Leo started to walk up and down the hall, and tried to think about playing croquet instead of thinking about using the bathroom. He wondered if he'd be able to beat his uncle too, and he figured that he probably would. Then he wondered if maybe there was some other place he could take a crap, like in a bucket, and then get rid of it later, but then he heard a flush and the door finally opened and his uncle came out.

"The picture album's on the shelf in the living room," said Leo.

"Sure," said his uncle.

It smelled terrible in the bathroom, but Leo went in and sat down on the toilet right away. The seat was warm and there were brown bits of Mr. Tibbs' hair on the pink and white linoleum floor. Leo leaned forward and closed his eyes, his shoulders resting on his bare, skinny knees, and he tried to imagine what it would be like to do cocaine. He wondered if it was like playing a really good game of croquet, but then he thought it had to be even better than that. He thought it might feel like taking 500 dumps all at once while driving down the 401 on a Harley while a girl in a bikini was watching you. He decided he'd be willing to spend all of his birthday money to give that a try.

He was in the bathroom for a while. He used a lot of toilet paper and it took two flushes to get it all down. When he went back downstairs the photo album was still sitting on the shelf and his uncle wasn't there. He took the album off the shelf and sat down on the carpet and flipped through the pages until he found the picture of him and his uncle and his uncle's custom Harley. The colours were fading into yellow and green, but Leo thought it was still a pretty good shot and he peeled back the clear cellophane from the page and held the picture in his hands. The bike was low with handlebars that went up high with leather tassels on the end, and the gas tank had a skull and a lightning bolt painted on it. His uncle had told him what kind of Harley it was and what kind of engine it had, but Leo could never remember. The bike was parked on an angle in the driveway and Uncle Oscar wore black jeans and a black motorcycle jacket with red padded shoulders and he held Leo up in front of the bike. Leo wore a diaper and his blue T-shirt was riding up so that his belly was showing. His uncle had one arm underneath Leo's bum and legs and with his other hand he was holding the motorcycle helmet on Leo's head. Leo's hands were balled into little fists and the helmet was way too big for Leo, so that his whole face was showing through the hole in the front, and he was grinning. His uncle looked younger, and he was smiling too, like he was very happy, and Leo wondered if it was because he was pleased to be holding his nephew or if it was his new bike or a mixture of the two.

Mr. Tibbs came and jumped in Leo's lap then, and Leo pushed him away. He got up and took the picture down to the basement but Uncle Oscar wasn't there. His uncle's boots were gone, but his guitar was still lying beside the chair where Leo had left it. Leo shoved the picture in his left pocket and went back upstairs and looked around and nothing else seemed to be missing. He went to the front door to check and found it open. He tried to remember if he'd locked it when he came home, but he couldn't be sure.

"Fuck," he said. He thought his uncle might have left a note on the kitchen table, but there wasn't one. For a moment he thought something bad might have happened to his uncle, but then he thought about it some more and decided he'd probably just left all of a sudden, so he wouldn't have to say goodbye.

Then Leo called his mother at DivaMax and told her how he'd let his uncle upstairs to use the washroom, and how they'd planned to go to the parkette and how Uncle Oscar had left. She didn't say anything at first, and then she sighed, deeply, and he couldn't tell whether it was him she was disappointed in, or his uncle. Then he told her he'd told Francesco about Uncle Oscar, but that Francesco didn't seem to care, and his mother told him it didn't matter, that he shouldn't worry. He felt like he had to say something else. He didn't know what else to say, so he said, "Ramon's a drug dealer."

His mother was silent for a second, and then she said, "Why did you tell me that, Leo?"

"Because it's true," he said. "What are we going to do about Uncle Oscar?"

"It's okay, Leo," she said. "We'll find out where he's gone when I get home."

"Okay." Leo hung up the phone. His mother hadn't sounded as angry as he'd expected and this made him feel guilty, as if he'd been the one who'd done something wrong, and not his uncle. He went to the living room window, and peered out through the drapes. The sky looked very grey but he felt like he couldn't just sit there and wait for his mom to come home. He knew he'd start to go crazy and his asthma would act up, and that the only thing to do was to go to the parkette and play croquet by himself. That was the only thing that would help him relax. He looked out of the window again. It was going to rain for sure.

When he stopped at the front closet to put on his raincoat, Mr. Tibbs came running up and rubbed himself against the door like he did whenever he was upset about something.

Usually Mr. Tibbs didn't like people at all, and Leo couldn't understand why the cat liked his uncle so much. He picked up Mr. Tibbs in both hands and looked him in the face and said, "Why did you let him get away?" and when the cat meowed and squirmed and pawed at his face, Leo threw him feet first towards the couch. Then he went outside as quickly as he could and locked the door behind him. Immediately his raincoat felt heavy and sticky against his neck and the bare skin of his arms. "Fuck it," he said, and set his croquet set down and took off his raincoat like it was a pain in the ass. He bunched it up and shoved it inside the mailbox and then picked up his croquet set again and headed towards the park. When he came to the corner, Ramon was still there, sitting in the Camaro ss. It was not until Leo was halfway across the street that Ramon called out to him.

"Hey," said Ramon. "You come back for what we talked about before?"

"I'm going to the park," said Leo, refusing to look back over his shoulder.

"It's gonna rain," said Ramon.

Leo tried to shrug to show he didn't care, but the croquet set weighed him down so he couldn't lift his shoulders. He kept walking, and didn't even turn to look when he heard the car door open.

"Slow down," Ramon called out, but it wasn't until Leo felt the hand upon his shoulder that he stopped and turned to face him. He couldn't remember the last time he'd seen Ramon get out of his car. Ramon was much taller than he remembered, almost a whole foot taller than Leo, and his long black T-shirt and baggy jeans hung loosely on his limbs.

"You got that money?" said Ramon.

"What money?" said Leo.

"What you packing in that case?" said Ramon, and Leo did not reply.

"Show me," said Ramon. Ramon reached for the croquet set then, and Leo pulled away, though he knew it was pointless to resist. Ramon placed his hand upon Leo's wrist and wrenched the handle from him while Leo forced himself not to cry out in pain. Then Ramon knelt down on the sidewalk, held the case against his bent leg, and opened the latches. "What the fuck," he said, as he looked inside, and then he turned the case upside down, dumping its contents onto the sidewalk. The mallet heads and the shafts and wickets and balls all fell onto the cement and the balls started to roll away. He took off his ball cap and held it in his hand and ran his fingers through his short, slick hair and stood there, surveying the pile at his feet. Then he put his hat back on and reached down and picked up one of the shafts and the green ball. He threw the ball up in the air and swung at it like it was a baseball. He missed and the ball rolled into the gutter and Leo chased after it. He heard a cracking sound behind him and when he turned he saw Ramon holding half of a broken shaft in each hand, his right knee still raised in the air.

"We had a deal," said Ramon.

"We never had a deal," said Leo. He felt anger well within him, his cheeks growing red and hot with a deep hatred, as much for his uncle as for Ramon. He reached down and picked up the green ball then, felt the cold, heavy roundness of it in his hand, and he threw it at Ramon with all his force. The ball hit the tarmac fifteen feet from its target, rolled off the street and came to rest in a curb-side storm drain. Ramon stood there and smiled, just as he had done earlier that afternoon. He looked down again at the wickets and shafts and mallet heads on the sidewalk before him, nudged the pile of equipment with the toe of his sneaker. He crouched down and picked up another shaft and a mallet head and examined them closely.

"I see how this shit goes together," he said, and he twisted the mallet head onto the end of the shaft. Then he lifted the mallet high in the air, as if to pound a stake into the ground, and when he brought it down upon the lid of the case Leo heard something snap.

"Fuck off," Leo screamed.

"I'll take whatever you got on you," said Ramon, "and we'll call it even." Leo's chest constricted and he felt the hotness of tears running down his cheeks. He reached into his pocket for his puffer, but it wasn't there. Instead he felt the crispness of the two twenty dollar bills and he didn't know what else to do so he went up to Ramon and handed them to him. Ramon took the bills and slid them into his pocket without looking at them, and then he dropped the mallet on the ground. Leo watched him for a moment, and struggled to breathe deeply and slowly. Ramon looked back at him, impassive, as if nothing out of the ordinary had happened. It occurred to Leo that he had not been given anything in exchange for his $40 and it was clear to him then that Ramon had never intended to sell him anything. He knew his mother would ask him how he'd spent the money, and he did not know what he'd say.

Gradually, his panic receded and he bent down and turned over the case and started to pick up the scattered wickets and he tried to forget about his anger and his shame so that he could focus on the task at hand. He was conscious of Ramon standing over him, watching him, and he wondered how his actions could be of any interest to Ramon, now that Ramon had taken what he wanted. He looked up at Ramon then, as if daring him to speak, knowing that whatever Ramon could possibly say would only cause greater humiliation. Ramon said nothing. Instead he turned from Leo and went over to the storm drain and stooped to pick up the green ball and came back and handed it to him. Then Ramon went over to the edge of the sidewalk and picked up two shafts that had rolled away, returned and knelt beside Leo, and placed the shafts in their slots in the case and the two of them worked together until the case was almost full. One of the case's hinges was broken and so was the handle, and when Leo stood up he had to hold it in his arms to keep it shut. Ramon stood facing him, arms crossed. His sudden kindness only embarrassed Leo and when Ramon nodded towards his Camaro ss and said, "I'll give you a ride to the park," Leo did not know at first how he should respond.

He realized then that Ramon did not have anything against him, that Ramon was obligated to steal from him because he was weak, just as his Uncle Oscar was bound to hurt him and his mother because they had been foolish enough to care. Leo wondered if his uncle had ever bought drugs from Ramon, wondered if Ramon had seen his uncle pass by that afternoon. He thought about his uncle selling his custom Harley, wondered if the bike had meant anything to whoever had bought it, if that person felt anything like what his uncle had felt on the day the picture had been taken. It occurred to Leo that just as easily as he'd given away his birthday money he might reach into his left pocket and take out the photo of his uncle and show it to Ramon. Ramon might recognize his uncle. Leo thought that when his mom found out where Uncle Oscar had gone he could tell Ramon, and if Ramon did not care about where his uncle had gone, he would know someone who did. Then Leo thought he might like to play croquet with Ramon, if only to defeat him, that Ramon might even agree to play croquet against him if he asked him now, but Leo knew this was something else that he would never do.

"No thanks," said Leo, and as soon as he said this he knew it would have been better if he'd said nothing at all. Ramon shrugged and turned and went and got inside his car. Leo started back down the street towards the park and he heard the engine turn over behind him and then Ramon drove by slowly and grinned and waved at him as he turned the corner and Leo did not wave back.

He was almost at the parkette when he heard the first rumble of thunder. He watched for lightning, but there wasn't any. The parkette was deserted except for an old man wearing a brown suit and an old-fashioned black hat with a brim. The man sat on the park bench with his hands on his knees and watched Leo set up the wickets, but as soon as the rain started the man got up and opened his umbrella and slowly walked away. The parkette was just a slide and a swing set that Leo used to play on when he was younger. There were two fir trees, and some flowers, and a good patch of grass there too, and it was flat. Leo set the wickets up far apart and at odd angles to make the shots as difficult as he could. The rain came down hard and fast, and he was soaked to the skin before he even started the game. His feet felt swollen and heavy and squished inside his sneakers. The rain made him need to piss, but he forced himself to ignore the tension in his bladder. He imagined that the raindrops were thousands of tiny wet fists, all pelting him with blows, trying to keep him from playing the game, and that he did not care about them because they could not really hurt him. He decided to use the green ball and he set it down next to the starting stake. He aimed for the first wicket and came up short. He didn't make it through until the third stroke. It wasn't easy to make the ball go where he wanted because it was wet and so was the grass, and it was hard for him to see, but he was determined to complete the course before he packed up and went home. He wondered if it was raining in Mississauga too. He thought the soccer game would be called for sure and he knew the team would be disappointed, because they liked playing in the rain. He wondered where Francesco was, if he was with Isabel, and what they were doing. Leo was shivering by the time he made it through the seventh wicket and lined up to hit the turning stake. He nailed the shot and the ball bounced off and rolled back towards the seventh wicket, as if he'd planned it that way.

The second half of the game went by much faster. He'd stopped shivering and nothing bothered him at all. Someone could be watching, he thought, a stranger, or his mother or his Uncle Oscar or Ramon even, and he wouldn't even notice. When he made it back through the second wicket, he realized that at some point he had stopped keeping track of his strokes. But when he hit the first stake again and ended the game, he knew he'd done pretty well, that he'd played some of the best croquet he'd ever played. The rain had almost stopped completely. He looked up at the sky and it was still grey, but not as dark as before, though it was almost evening. As he packed the wickets in the case he thought he should probably towel them off when he got home, so they wouldn't rust, and dry his mallet so it wouldn't warp, and he was glad that he had thought of this before it was too late.

Now that he was finished playing he became aware again of how badly he needed to piss. He always needed to piss when he'd been out in the rain for a while, especially when he wasn't wearing his raincoat and his clothes got wet. It was as if the rain seeped right through his skin and filled him up until it felt like he would burst. He knew he wouldn't make it home before he pissed himself. He looked around the park and up and down the street and there was still no one around. He went over and stood between the two fir trees, which were only slightly taller than he was, their branches heavy and drooping with rain. When he unzipped his pants his underwear was soaking wet, and his dick was shrivelled from the damp and the cold. The piss felt warm as it flowed out of him and steam rose up from the wet grass. It felt like he was standing there pissing for a very long time, like it would never end.

DANIELLE EGAN

PUBLICITY

Here she comes. She's barely a woman and could be mistaken for one of the tennis stars on my flight, what with the tracksuit and long blonde ponytail and running shoes that look like UFOs. But the eyes are a giveaway. She has the eyes of a handler. Already.

"I'm Lana. Good to meet you!" She smiles with her mouth but doesn't commit the eyes.

"Hello, Lana. Thanks for coming." Probably didn't have a choice, poor girl. After what's happened, they might have sent someone older.

"The car's right out front," she says, going for my bag, which I give up too easily. She leads the way, generating a current that smells of soap. "How was the flight?"

"Turbulent." My body still feels poised to leap from its skin.

"Sorry." As if she could have done anything about it.

Her car resembles a large shiny bike helmet. It's an effort to climb up and in.

"Go," she says, and the vehicle starts moving without making a sound.

"Welcome back," says a voice from the dashboard, sounding slightly wistful.

The highway looks brand new, with partially finished off-ramps leading nowhere. I'm desperate to see the mountains, but huge electronic billboards line the route, hawking resorts, casinos, water parks – all branded The One & Only.

"I haven't been back here since 1985."

"Then you'll notice a lot of changes!"

At least the mountains will still be there, trailing off into the water. Those giant green blobs that appear when I conjure up my old life with Sarah, at the beginning.

"Sorry about that *E-Life* piece last night. We didn't see it coming."

"Neither did I." I should have seen it coming the moment I laid eyes on Sibby running on tiptoes into the Sulu Sea. I should have had the guts to look away, to take the first flight home to Sarah, hang up this whole sordid writing thing once and for all.

"The publisher and your agent have been trying to reach you."

"I lost my phone," I lie. I tossed it in the Chicago River after my lawyer emailed me the tabloid show's incriminating spot: the grainy security footage of Sibby and me entering my hotel together, halfway round the world, and the book critic calling my new novel a "pallid imitation of *Lolita*." All timed to broadcast around the globe and just in time for Publicity.

"The interview requests doubled overnight. They want to set you up with a PR coach."

"That won't be necessary." I don't have the stamina or the patience to practise for the onslaught.

"It's almost over. Two more sleeps." She gives me a conspiratorial we're-in-this-thing-together grin. But then, handlers are paid to be onside. How did she fall into this damn PR game anyway?

The city rears up and I want to gasp at the sheer volume of skyscrapers. Publicity: Population 7,846,801 and growing by the nanosecond. Even the mountains are jam-packed right to the top with housing, save for the jagged peaks.

"What have they done to the mountains?" The hysteria in my tone startles the onboard computer.

"Do you need assistance, Lana?" asks the voice.

"No. Sleep," she says to the dashboard, then to me, "It happened so fast, starting with the 2/13 terrorist attacks in LA and New York during the Olympics. We were supposed to get hit too, but the city was crawling with security."

"I remember the news clips of cruise ships full of rent-a-cops."

"Yeah, they're still here."

"The ships or the cops?"

"Both. Together. A lot of people stayed on after the airports and borders reopened, and more have been pouring in ever since the Saudi-American war started. We needed somewhere to put everyone, including all those actors and athletes that refuse to work anywhere else. It's never too hot here, and other than the odd flash flood, it doesn't rain much anymore."

It rained non-stop those first days Sarah and I were here. Sometimes we couldn't even see the houses across the street, and the sound of foghorns was the only reminder that there were other people around.

"Who is this Lucky Woods character on all of the bill-boards and bus stops?"

"She's a local real-estate tycoon. Owns The One & Only development company. She'll probably be our mayor next year."

"At least she's prettier than Stalin."

"She's had a lot of cosmetic surgery." Lana grins with her eyes this time, and it's such a lovely sight that I can't resist smiling back.

She stops at a toll bridge and flashes a laminated card. "They restrict downtown car traffic now." The bridge feeds into a tall canyon of skyscrapers that frames those slashed-up mountains, but she turns, loops under the bridge, and comes up alongside the bay and a recreational highway, with its bike, rollerblade, and walking lanes in heavy use. Where did the old seawall go, with its crumbly stairs disappearing under the waterline? The logs are still there, lined up for the sunbathers. The water looks so cool and inviting.

"Can you still swim in there?"

"Of course."

"Nobody's swimming."

"There's an indoor pool at your hotel."

I don't want a pool. I want to swim in that bay, where I asked Sarah to marry me and she said yes, put her cool arms around my neck and kissed me with her hot mouth.

The pastel Miami-style apartments still line the beachside avenue, but are mixed with taller, sleek glass towers. Many of the balconies are packed with people, drinking cocktails, looking out at the water and the impending sunset, as if in theatre boxes watching a performance. Parked on the bay are dozens of yachts, a high-end floating shantytown.

"What are all those boats doing here?"

"Most of them anchor here year-round, but some are here for the fireworks tomorrow."

"What's the occasion?"

"Nothing special. They happen *every* Friday."

With the mountains all carved up, this place isn't as electrifyingly green as I remember, although colours tend to ripen in the memory bank. After Sarah left me for good last year, I got the greens of this place all mixed up with her eyes, but when she finally agreed to see me again a few weeks ago, they seemed so dull and translucent as she said, "I wish I just felt like I don't know you anymore. What you've *become*. But now I wonder if I ever really knew you at all."

What possessed me to think that she wouldn't suspect the story was anything more than fiction? And then to look her in the eyes and feign shock at the very suggestion? I should have burned that manuscript, but hubris brought me here instead.

"Here we are," says Lana, as if to a toddler needing the loo.

The hotel is a tall, impossibly thin glass slab plunked like a gravestone atop the old Sylvia Hotel, where Sarah and I once drank too many Long Island iced teas. We pass by an army of paparazzi and crowds of people waiting for a glimpse of some celebrity or other. Lana pulls into the roundabout. A bellhop comes jogging over, grinning wildly, the eager eyes of a fan.

"It's a huge honour to meet you, sir. I'm Marius." He grabs my bag from Lana and leads the way into the lobby and the elevator, past blankly curious eyes, the odd pair flashing with a tabloid-induced hatred of recognition.

Marius blurts out, "I'm a huge fan. I've read everything." He presses 39 and keeps his finger on the button. "I just have to say, that *E-Life* piece last night was an abomination. I hope you sue the crap out of them." His anger is better than pity, or the horrific nudge-wink of my lawyer.

"Here we are," says Lana, before the elevator doors have even slid open. She must be desperate to get to cocktails on balconies, away from this sordid handler job.

The room is full of gift baskets, mostly fruit. Who could ever eat all this fruit? I'd have to hunker down and make a full-time job of it.

The bay is a sheet of pale blue with the sun gone down. But still nobody swimming. Is it contaminated? I'm desperate to get my stinking shoes off, but not until they leave. "Please take a basket, both of you. I insist."

They pick a small basket each.

"My number's on the schedule," says Lana. "Don't hesitate to call."

"See you bright and early." I wave, but they're too close to be waved at, and the gesture feels somehow violent.

Sleep is impossible and eventually I crack.

"Are you sure you can swim in there?"

"Ah, yes."

"Oh, did I wake you?" Or maybe I interrupted something else.

"No. I'm awake. I'll call the hotel and tell them to give you after-hours privileges at the pool."

"I don't want the pool."

"The bay's clean. I'm positive."

"Do you swim in it?"

"I'm not much of a swimmer. I'll make a call and –"

"No please. I shouldn't have called. I should be sleeping. You should be sleeping. I don't have a swimsuit anyway."

"I'll get you one."

"You're very sweet, but that's not necessary. I'm off to bed now. Goodbye. Sorry."

Under the bathroom's greenish interrogational light, I face off against my pasty, saggy, cellulite-pocked body. I know what lurks below the surface, having seen too many televised lipo-suctions: the unconscious body on the metal slab, vivisected by scalpels, the slashed flaps assaulted by a screeching vacuum that suctions out a milkshake of nicotine-coloured fat and pink capillaries. The sad, vulgar vulnerability of imperfection laid out for the world's entertainment.

Here in Publicity, even the toilets refuse to mind their own business. An indifferent voice intones: "Low potassium and pH levels and high specific gravity. Please increase intake of fruits, vegetables, complex carbohydrates and water."

Here she comes, a skyscraper of coffee in hand, looking for me with that circumspect gaze. Who knows what kind of new scandal I'm capable of getting into under her watch? She wears a tangerine suit and heels, high and noisy on the marble.

I stand up and wave, and she smiles at me with her bright-orange mouth.

"Good morning. I hope you slept well."

"Yes, thanks," I lie. She sits down, giving off a waft of soap. Is it a kind of perfume? Fingernails painted orange, too. Were they like that yesterday? "Sorry about last night."

"It's no problem." She gives a between-you-and-me smile, then makes a grabbing motion across the screen of the lobby bar's E-Paper, as if to ball up its contents.

"It's okay. I've already seen it." The new footage of a small but noisy group of picketers in front of a BookMart, wanting me stripped of my Booker Prize, while a couple of free-speechers attempt to drown them out.

"You'll do the TV and digital-streaming interviews in Conference Room 25, and we have a backup room for print journalists if we start running behind. Oh, and we might have to evacuate. There's a wildfire heading west. Nothing serious right now, but the winds could change."

"There was nothing in the paper about *that*."

"I checked about the hotel pool. You can swim any time you like. Just call the concierge. There are swimsuits in the store downstairs. Not very fashionable, unfortunately."

Bless her for pretending it matters.

"Still nobody swimming out there."

She checks her watch. "It's early."

"But look at all the people on the beach, in *swimsuits*."

"I'm sure they'll go swimming."

There's that make-it-happen voice again. She'd need to hire actors or bribe people.

"How did the interviews go?"

"Fine." I was an utter fool to pass up the warm-up coaching.

"Ready for the next one?"

"Yes." Even if it kills me.

She beckons to a young woman, in pigtails of all things.

"I'd like to smoke," I say.

"I didn't know you smoked." Lana sounds offended, not by the habit but because she should have known. "You can't smoke in the hotel. You can't really smoke anywhere."

"Then we'll go to my room." I can keep my eyes on the water. "We'll eat some fruit, okay?" I say to the journalist, who shrugs and smirks. Obviously not a fan. Probably just a hack reporter, looking for a break, baiting herself for the tabs.

Lana accompanies us right to the door of my suite. She seems to disapprove of my bringing this reporter to my room. Is everything suspect now?

Pigtails admits upfront that she's not read any of my books. She's familiar only with the ones made into movies, so there's no safe reminiscing about favourite fictional characters, as if they have minds of their own and are still out there doing their own thing; if only they'd just call and check in once in a while to let you know they're okay.

"Did you pick the Philippines knowing that the age of consent there is only 12?"

I resist the urge to hiss, *Get your facts straight. She was 15!* Almost 17 now. "I went there to write about a *fictional* marine biologist investigating mass dolphin beachings," I say instead.

"So, *it* just happened by accident? Like manslaughter?"

Lana's decisive knock is right on time.

"The air conditioning is too cold," I snap before she's even had the chance to close the door on Pigtails. "I need to get outside!"

"Fine. Why don't you do the next one at the beach? It's just audio."

Yes, I'll let the sun penetrate my surface-of-the-moon skin until it's so hot, there's no choice but to go swimming. Before it's too late. Before I go home, where there's no natural, unspoiled body of water left. Another regret would be too heavy for the plane.

As we pass the phalanx of cameras camped outside, representing the worst of the tabs – CNN, TRUMP, and TMZ – Lana puts a protective hand on my shoulder for a second before thinking twice and taking it off. I feel like a spurned child.

The CBC reporter shakes my hand. "I'm a big fan of your work," he says, as if confessing guilt by association.

"Do you swim in there?" He looks like he could do anything with that body. They all look like they're in training for something.

"Ah. I'm not really into swimming."

"Do you smell smoke?"

"No," the reporter and Lana answer in unison, as if a natural disaster would reflect badly on *them*.

We yield to the traffic on the recreational highway and run for our lives when there's a break. "I've got lunch for you," says Lana, handing me a canvas bag. Her eyes are hidden behind large black sunglasses, but her rosy cheeks ball up encouragingly.

The reporter wants to go way back in time and talk about his favourite character, Piggy La Fleur, on his doomed honeymoon. "I loved that scene where he's trapped in the hotel's glass elevator, in his Speedo. He panics and tries to climb up to the hatch, but he's all greasy with suntan oil. People below are pointing and laughing and he spots his new bride looking mortified and he realizes that she doesn't really love him. You make the most terrible things so funny."

Have I always been such a plunderer, exploiting the vulnerable for a cheap laugh? If only I could swim! I need to be submerged, cleansed, exfoliated with sea salt. The breeze is so hot and the paved mountains seem to heave and smother, providing no relief.

"I'm having trouble reconciling this place with the one I remember."

"When were you here last?"

"Thirty-five years ago. It was raining and the whole city was socked in, so we had no clue there were mountains everywhere. We woke up one morning and there they were, as if they'd sprung up out of our dreams. We had to go swimming before we could believe they were real. It's terrible, what they've done to the mountains."

"The One & Only has built a lot of affordable housing up there. And everybody gets a crack at owning one through the lottery. There's a $7 million dollar home up this week."

Three children running for the water! They run right in without hesitation, kicking through small waves and shrieking from the cold shock. How wonderful it must feel. Who cares if the water's tainted? I should stand up right now, expose this rotting body and jump in. I'll keep swimming towards those mirage-like green mountains in the distance, until I'm too tired to fight off life.

I'll do it. I must. I'll tear off my shirt and make a run for it. But what if I find the shoreline covered with scummy debris and chicken out? What if a shooter gets a picture of decrepit old me lurking near the children? How readily accessible is the lurid tabloid version of the self, turning even the most innocent yearnings to shit.

"I thought you might cancel after that piece on *E-Life*." That hadn't even occurred to me. Am I just a monkey on a leash? Or so much worse? "If it's any consolation, I think it's your best book."

"Thank you." I wish I didn't feel the same way.

Here comes Lana to collect her charge. "Did you see those kids swimming?" she asks.

"Yes. They were speaking German though." Probably tourists, and tourists don't know any better. They'll swim in anything.

She shepherds me into the hotel through a service entrance, alongside tiny Asian maids and Amazonian actresses.

"You're sunburned," says Lana, inspecting my face with concern. She roots through her bag for a bottle of aloe gel. "This will soothe your skin," she says, and my throat starts to burn with the threat of childish tears at the shock of maternal attention. It's something of a relief to know that, on an autonomic level, I can still react to kindness.

But it leaves me vulnerable for the next interview, another TV crew, tanned and armoured with muscles. How do they find the time, here in Publicity?

"Forty-five minutes," she says to them. She's developing frown lines already.

I perspire heavily under the blinding television lights, which I suspect suits them fine. They've brought no one to powder my nose or remind me not to wear stripes.

"You've always been drawn to the theme of exploitation, but critics are saying you've taken the subject too far," says the reporter, licking his lips. "Do you think your *protagonist* committed a crime?"

"Yes."

"In some countries he'd get life in prison."

"Here, in so-called civilized countries, they rarely even do time. We express outrage, but we do nothing to change the laws."

"So this book is meant to highlight our cultural hypocrisies? Express that we're all somehow complicit in child rape?"

I lie about needing to go to the bathroom, which will surely be perceived as a glaring indication of guilt.

Lana is hovering outside. "Where are you going?"

"It's horrible. I just want to go swimming!"

"I can arrange that."

"I don't want you to *arrange* anything. Just let me go to the fucking bathroom!"

"Of course," she says, stepping back. I'm disappointing her too.

"Why do we do this?" I mutter to my big, sunburned clown face in the mirror. How could twenty minutes outdoors wreak such havoc? The bags under my eyes glow a sickly bluish-white from wearing sunglasses, and there are grim white creases around my nasolabial folds. Why didn't she tell me how awful I look? I'd like to retreat to a dark crawl space to die, but she's pacing outside waiting for me.

"Okay?"

"I survived. I'm sorry for –"

"I understand. Just two more today and no more cameras, I promise."

"I'll do them at the bar. You should take a break." Somebody should be looking out for her, too.

"We'll head to your reading at six."

"You must have better things to do."

"Like fireworks?" She smiles with her whole face, and it's like a life preserver.

Here she comes, black sleeveless dress, black stilettos, hair spilling around her shoulders. Does she have a room here for quick changes? The nails are still orange. That's reassuring.

"There's been a bomb threat at the venue. We had to cancel the public reading."

"Oh dear." So it's come to this.

"Don't worry. It was probably something to do with that action movie about the Saudi-American war. It premieres tonight at the multiplex next door. But we've found a new venue for a private reading."

She looks unimpressed when I order a double, and starts clock-watching when my bellboy fan Marius and his hugely pregnant and famished girlfriend join us. By the time the bill arrives, we're fifteen minutes behind schedule.

"I'm paying. I insist," I say. Lana doesn't put up a fight.

Walking to the reading, we hit an intersection clogged with environmentalist protesters and riot police. I think there might still be hope for this town, but it turns out to be a movie shoot. Within two blocks there's another movie shoot; it's hard to tell where the real world begins.

The new venue is a cramped condominium party room.

Aside from a few very attractive young people who look like movie extras, there's a murder of book-chain execs, old-fart academics, and errant realtors. I stick with a safe passage about the mass dolphin suicides, and get the reading done before the slurring kicks in.

Afterwards, there's a little party for me in a condo on the 52nd floor – one of those cold, modern, blinding-white jobs, full of wilting food in takeout containers and boxes of wine. Lana stays in the background, ever-watchful, throwing me the occasional guarded glance. The talk is mostly bestseller lists, government grants, books about war, finance, science – real life, that's what everyone wants. Nobody trusts fiction anymore, and why should they?

I escape downstairs for a cigarette. Out on the street, I realize that I left the pack in my jacket and that I'm locked out of the condo. Locked out of my own party, surely my last.

Eventually, three young men exit the building. I'm grabbing for the door when one of them tells me who I am. A fan that had tickets to the cancelled reading. "Remember when Dumbbell Moynihan called in the bomb threat at his orthodontist's office?" he says. As if it's possible to forget any of your characters.

He lights up a large joint and proceeds to tell his friends the tale of Dumbbell at the prom, in his too-tight yellow tuxedo with his "big fat date." He exaggerates, skips and skews a number of important things, but I'm too busy sucking in huge drags to fact-check. I even laugh along with them until he calls Dumbbell's math teacher "Mrs. Asslicker," and I have to break in and say, "Mrs. Aisslicher."

That just makes them roar harder, and it suddenly smacks of a sitcom laugh track. Is my life's work just puerile stoner comedy, like so many sad clowns pouring out of a tiny car? And why drag poor Dumbbell and his childhood sweetheart into it? She wasn't fat, just big-boned! Oh, you ridiculous old cretin, exploiting everyone and everything that is good and sincere for the entertainment of complete strangers.

I can't even trust my fans. I might even hate them.

Back upstairs, I'm very stoned and very paranoid, so I get into the food, mostly just broccoli stems left for me – at *my* party! Then the last box of wine, and soon I'm babbling and snorting, flirting with the one other drunken person in the room: a cashier from the bookstore with a slight moustache and long, fake white fingernails.

Lana, meanwhile, sits statue-straight in the corner, sipping water, stifling yawns. Why doesn't she go home! I don't need a babysitter! Then there's a window-shaking blast and I flinch and duck, thinking, *the bombers have found me!* But it's just the fireworks starting, and I've spilled red wine all over the place, which has the impact of a bloody explosion and the scene goes into crisis mode.

On the way out, the irate hostess shoves the box of wine at me and slams the door in my face as I mutter apologies. Lana tries to take the wine away, but I'm not having any of it. I'll carry this albatross! The fresh air and the boom of fireworks sobers me up enough to realize how utterly fucked-up I am.

"I drank too much. I'm sorry."

"No, please. That was *awful*. We had such a nice party planned at an Indian restaurant near the original venue." She senses this could be my last.

"Why do you do this PR job?"

"I've been told I have the right personality for it."

"Meaning?"

"I'm not really interested in celebrities, to tell you the truth. Which allows me to be professional and gives me a necessary hostility towards the media."

Yes, the protectiveness. It's not for us, per se, it's against them.

"Of course I always read up before a job. I couldn't put your book down." She throws me a between-us look, but it strikes me as a much darker, more intimate collusion that sends a chill up my spine. We've reached the hotel lobby and the front-desk people are eyeing us.

"What did you think?"

"I think I'll walk you to the elevator and say goodnight."

I don't care if I wake her. "I heard that they closed the beaches here."

"Who told you that?"

"Why take it personally?"

"That was a long time ago."

"Two summers ago."

"It's late." She's not even trying to hide her irritation.

"I woke you."

"Yes."

"So you *can* tell the truth."

Silence at her end. She should say, "Fuck off old man." She could say anything to me.

"You despise me."

"I don't."

"What if it had happened to you?"

"Look, this isn't appropriate."

"Please. Oh god, just never mind. I'm sorry. Good night."

My hands are trembling so much that I can barely hang up the phone. Everything good is lost and I shall surely die alone, unloved and undeserving. The phone rings.

"It did happen to me. I was twelve. Years younger than Sibby."

It's a shock to hear the name out loud.

"My parents had just divorced. He was my mother's boyfriend."

"Did you tell your mother?"

"I've never told anyone."

"Why?"

"I don't know. It was a long time ago. My life is more than that. It has to be."

"Did you hate him?"

She says nothing for a long time. I feel as if my entire being exists only as energy that will be snuffed out as soon as the connection is broken.

"Sometimes, later, I wished I had hated him, but I liked his attention. I wanted to see where it would go. It was my curiosity I kind of hated later. He didn't force me to do anything."

"How do you know that? They say that . . ." I can't say it. It's too awful.

"They *groom* you. Yes, he probably did and I'm certainly not excusing him. But I groomed him too. I could sense it in him."

"Sense what?"

"That he was vulnerable."

I don't want to hear anything else, but she's right about curiosity. Once it starts, it can't easily be stopped.

"His attention was sort of repellant, but I liked it. I felt powerful for the first time in my life. Later, my views changed. But you can't rewrite the way you feel. Not even with fiction."

"But that's why it's such a terrible *crime*. You could still do something about it!"

"It would be easier if it was black and white. But that doesn't change anything for either of us, does it? I'm not going to say any more."

The line goes dead.

I want to cry, and not being able to makes me feel oddly emasculated, impotent. I go outside to pace the beach. In the dark, the mountains dance with lights and seem restored, at least until sunrise. The moon is a bright yellow crescent hanging over the yacht-littered water. It looks like a movie prop.

A man wearing a T-shirt emblazoned "The One & Only" approaches and asks, "Spare five bucks for the house lottery?"

"Do you swim in the bay?"

"Never learned how, buddy."

"I'll give you $20 if you wade around in it for a while."

"Go fuck yourself, you old perv," he yells and stalks off.

I go to the water's edge, trying to will myself into the water. But even my desire to enter it has become utterly embarrassing. I just can't swim with me there watching, judging, taking notes, ruining everything.

Even sleep abandons me, and who could blame it? I wait in the lobby for the clothing store to open. Lana was right about the meagre selection of swim trunks. I choose long Hawaiian shorts in garish colours. They bulge under my pants but give me a semblance of courage to face the last day.

Here she comes, in a white suit and such precarious matching shoes that I tense up watching her approach. Her face is mask-like with heavy makeup, which makes her look older, more weathered somehow. Or maybe it's the new knowledge weighing down my impression. She's already accompanied by the day's first reporter, so there's no small talk about sleep, no consolatory attempts to fend off the latest onslaught of media hate, no room for my lame apologies. For the final inquisition, she even leaves me in the hot seat for an extra twenty minutes, my mesh-ensconced scrotum sweating profusely and the plastic-knobbed price tag knifing into my side.

"You're done," she says afterwards, meaning who knows what.

"I'm going to swim in that bay. I want to go to Spanish Banks." Where my life began, with such joy and promise.

"Fine." She doesn't believe me. "We'll stop en route to the airport. I'll handle the checkout while you get your stuff."

Ten minutes later, I barely have a chance to close the passenger door before she starts driving. She drives too fast and I feel a paternalistic desire to scold her.

"Why did you take this gig? I'm not a celebrity."

"You're listed on Celebrity.com."

What kind of a world put me there? But my disgust is overwhelmed by smug, unstoppable vanity.

"Nobody swimming. As usual."

She doesn't respond, just starts marching towards the shoreline.

"Look at all the brown froth."

"Well?" She crosses her arms and glares at me with unfettered hostility. Oh, Lana, it wasn't supposed to be like this.

"I don't think I can." It comes out barely a whisper.

"This is ridiculous," she says. She drops her bag, unbuttons her suit jacket and tosses it to the sand. She kicks off each shoe, then unzips her skirt and lets it drop down around her feet. Her underpants are white.

"Stop," I say, but only part of me wants her to stop. Next she removes her white camisole and flings it sideways, but it's so light that it gets caught in the breeze and takes forever to land, too close to the dirty tide. Her bra is white too.

She turns and strides into the water, puts her arms above her head and dives under. I feel so proud of her and my body contracts like a runner at the starting gate, ready to bolt in as well. But I hesitate. My feelings turn to envy, which fills me with shame and roots me down, leaving only the aching, useless longing to go backwards in time and make everything right. I close my eyes and there, waiting for me, are the brilliant greens and blues of such a long, long time ago.

THE LONGITUDE OF OKAY

The tone sounds and Katrin turns to the class.

"That fire?" she asks, squishing her brow in bewilderment.

"No, Miss. Fire's a beeping one."

"Oh."

"I think that's the intruder tone," says Cody – *Co-deeee*, as he pronounces it – from the back row. She raises an eyebrow. Listens.

"Should have read the memo, Miss."

Every class has a smartass. Hers comes in a T-shirt, tight as a leotard over his bench-press chest, that reads *Ultimate Fighting Champion, Southwest Regionals, Kick Ass '08*. Katrin cannot gauge Cody's cheekiness. He has a lazy eye. She never knows whether to smile or call him out.

She peeks. The hallway's empty but for Slobo, a math teacher. His face, prairie dog–curious, bobs out from the frame two doors up. A fellow memo truant. Katrin offers a sheepish wave. He smirks, shrugs, and pulls back into his classroom.

She lingers a second longer. With Slobo's head out of the way, she catches something that doesn't fit by the vending machine at the end of the hall – a crouching nimbus unfurling like bad weather. Katrin watches with queasy fascination. The dark blur becomes a figure; then the figure comes into focus. Five feet eight inches of stooping, luckless boyhood made tall with adrenaline turns towards her. In black combat boots, no less. Her first feeling is irritation. The horrid familiarity of it all. His right hand hangs heavy with the dull glint of metal.

Katrin's knees go weak. He's moving. She shuts the door, flicks off the lights, waves at the students. Her voice comes out as a pant, tentative and thin.

"Get down. Get back."

Somebody snickers. For a moment, she feels the concavity of her will; she wishes one of the boys with good shoulders – Cody? – would step forward and take charge, so she could crumple. This is not who you are, Katrin. You don't save the day.

Nobody moves. Her glance fastens on a roll of Scotch tape and that's enough to forestall her panic. She grabs it, runs back to the door, slaps an uncollected test – it was a pass – over the small window, and fastens it down with the tape. One defensive step, and there's no turning back.

"It's for real," somebody whispers. They stand up, chairs screech along the tiles.

"Push the desks back. Everybody in the far corner. There. Go!"

Now her voice is stronger, gale force even. There is swearing, jostling. She hears cellphones open. Click. Click. Click. Like a dog's toenails on ceramic tiles.

"No!"

She gestures – slapping her hands shut. Then she's pointing like a drill sergeant. I don't know who you are, she thinks. I don't know who this is.

"One person dials security. One person calls 911. The rest – off."

She'd read that memo after all. So why pretend? She glanced at it really, but didn't pin it primly to her cubicle like her colleagues, hurling it instead into the recycling bin, her one small rebellion against scare-mongering and bureaucracy.

The door won't lock. The bolt moves but won't catch in the frame. She tries once, twice, three times. Why didn't she think of this earlier? Of all things, how could she make the door an afterthought?

In her head, she hears Ariane's laughter – the true kind, straight from the belly when she plays with the dog – so unlike the helium twitter she uses with friends. How good, how right, some sounds seem.

The PA repeats its old news in long tones: a melancholic war drum. It is violated with a crack.

Peter's lips vibrating on the back of her neck, his horny humming of the CBC morning show jingle, as she breaks from sleep – how she'd miss such waking.

The taut spring releasing the hammer. The cartridge's back end slammed. Friction. A chamber-fed explosion, its wretched propulsion. Pow. She resents the intimacy of this new sound, the space it claims.

The shot rings near Slobo's class. She hopes his door is locked. Two girls are whimpering in the back of her room and another student says, *Shut the fuck up.*

She flips the teacher's desk at the front of the room so it is on its side, and shoves it against the door.

"The door won't lock."

She's not looking at them when she says it.

But when she turns, Warbly, a tall and awkward boy with a flutter of vestigial adolescence in his speech, is beside her. Him, of all people? He shoves another smaller desk against the door, nesting inside the larger desk. And then Ole Bill, an injured steelworker taking her class for disability retraining, is up. She can't waste a second on surprise. He stacks four chairs and pushes them against the flipped desk, dragging his bum leg with every step.

The first thump. Ole Bill drops to his knees. Warbly flattens himself against the whiteboard. Katrin scrambles under the smaller desks, so her weight pushes against the flipped desk and the door. Leaning into her shoulder, she sees Esam, her quietest student, stand up quickly, remove the belt from his jeans, loop it around the doorknob, and pull it tight into a slip knot. The doorway juts out slightly into the classroom, and Esam pushes his body into the corner the door's depth creates with the adjacent wall. He sits down, pulls the belt taut, braces his feet against the floor, so his entire body anchors a vector of opposing tension. Katrin is eye level with him. She can see the distended veins on his brown forearms, the weird calm of his face.

The thump repeats, more insistent. The doorknob rattles. She absorbs the small agonies of the huddled students, stifled cries, tight-throated inhalations, and a whiff of heartbreaking shame – somebody has shit. Katrin pours all her weight against the desk.

"Open up!"

Katrin imagines the fixed-eye vacancy of a video game shooter. The voice is loud and young. Impossibly young. And then, freighted with menace and cortisol, all of him heaves against the door. The thump smacks hard against Katrin's shoulder, the desk's underbelly scrapes her cheek. Rough wood. Ole Bill's stack of chairs tumbles. He sprawls out under them with a small groan. She kicks at them with her feet, digging him out. Warbly slides down the wall, wiggles Bill free and gathers him into the huddle. Esam yanks harder on the belt.

"Don't fuck with me."

Katrin hears the vocal cords ragged with rage and regrets again that she is middle-aged, that she is not strong, that she has let disappointment chip away at the better part of herself.

She thinks about the fulcrum of Peter's elbow, his knee, resting her head in the hinges of his body, feeling quiet and safe with her nose pressed into the spice of his unworried warmth.

She has never seen a semi-automatic. Yet Katrin instinctively knows the sound a handgun slide makes – the queer metallic sibilance – when it's pushed back, the hammer cocked. What she doesn't know are the physics of a propelled bullet – whether it can penetrate the thin metal and Styrofoam sandwich of the door plus her laminate desk before reaching her shoulder's tight, acidic flesh.

She wonders if Ariane will arrive home from school on the verge of tears again today – the small humiliations of phys. ed. and recess, the snubs on the bus ride home, her own reflection in passing windows building into a low pressure system that bursts in the vestibule by the coat hooks and the refurbished deacon's bench. Katrin wishes for a good day. Let someone – anyone – say something nice to her. The lustre of her hair. Her perfect homework.

It doesn't matter. He is already shooting. The bullets make a pinging thud against the door metal. Two. Three. Four. Five. She is a thickness of skin, sinew, and bone between the bullets and her students, without understanding her own risks. She regrets this. She is unfit for selflessness. She's all self – except that it's frozen in place.

Katrin is suddenly full of a hard aching for sweetness – her mother's pear pie with its buttered pastry, warm sugary fruit, a hint of cloves in the syrup. One bite, held against her teeth, left only room for pleasure in the world.

The small rectangle of glass. Katrin hears the smash of his handgun against it, followed by a shot. The glass shatters and tremolos like a harpsichord. Tinkling. Tinkling. Tinkling. Katrin watches the test she'd pasted to the door drop like Victory Parade flotsam. Warbly pulls the students, crawling and crab-walking, tears streaming down hunted faces, to the wall flush with the door.

Bullets come into the room, ricochet off the low cement walls, the greyed tile.

"I know you're in there, fucker. I'll get you."

Who? Which one of them has brought this on? Katrin wonders wildly if she has done the right thing. If the door were open, he'd come in, find his target. Perhaps there would be one dead. Not all.

She hears the bullet's whine and seconds later, a gasp, a recoil of fright. Giovanna, a large, pleasant girl, slumps away from the huddle, holding her upper arm. Carmine lava spurts from her good earthy flesh. Esam turns, takes one hand off the belt to reach for her.

"No!" Katrin hisses.

She gets on her belly, wiggling like a salamander over to the girl who sits grey-faced, gushing blood, in the thrall of her own frailty. She pulls Giovanna down low, sinks her palm against the wound to exert pressure. But blood leaks recklessly out, staining Katrin's fingers crimson.

The next shot ricochets off the wall above the heads of the huddling students. There is a cry of disbelief, of insult. The bullet falls beside Katrin and the bleeding girl. Katrin pulls her hand off the wound, kicks off her shoes, lies on her back, and squirms out of her leotards. Her butt cheeks press into the tiles' archeology of spit, grit, bootprints, and crumbs. The tile is cold against her bare flesh. She yanks her tights from her feet, rolls back onto her belly, and fashions a tourniquet for Giovanna's arm.

The whole time, she says, "You're okay. It's okay."

Sirens. They have been ringing in her ears.

Another shot. It splits the air outside the classroom but does not enter.

There is the sound of feet. There are voices. Katrin nods to Esam, who lets go of the belt and takes over the tourniquet.

"Stay down," she tells the students.

Katrin is the first to stand up. She is bare-legged, barefoot. The blood of her student soaks through her thin blouse to her skin. Bile – a hot sickening cud – worms up her throat. The voice that comes through the glass is older, authoritative.

"Police! It's okay. Open up!"

She looks over at the huddled students and meets the eyes of Cody. The squatting boy's face is ashen. He lets out a soft groan, then topples into the shoulder of the girl next to him in a dead faint. Katrin turns and begins to pull the chairs and desk away from the door.

Leave us be.

Peter answers the phone. He answers the door. Grey crescents pool under his eyes. He says please, please, she won't talk. Katrin regrets the sound of his voice – its polite roundness, its deferential pleading, its way of making her notice how all the edges of their existence have been rubbed away, rounded off, avoided.

She won't read the newspapers. But Peter clips. He clips. *The things they're saying about you*, he beams.

"Courageous. Brave. A her –"

She holds up a hand. Don't. *I won't hear it.* And he stops. Then the phone stops with him, before the week is out.

She spends whole days in the bedroom, knees pulled to her chest, girding herself against her own choices – down duvets, decorative pillows, thick towels, the devouring softness of her home. Her husband with his edgeless voice.

"Mom."

Ariane pushes open the bedroom door. Katrin studies her daughter's ridiculous slippers: shaggy defanged yetis. Pink, no less. Her thighs are too generous, too round for twelve years. This is her child? Seriously? The girl's shoulders curve over a fleshy continuum of breasts, the belly pushes against an outgrown T-shirt and busts out at the waist of her sweatpants. What kind of mother have I been? Katrin wonders.

The girl advances across the room, 165 pounds of reticence, and curls herself on the bed at Katrin's feet.

"Are you okay, Mom?"

The voice is sugared with need, the eyes moist. Katrin wants to slap her, slap her so hard the ample flesh splits and the young girl suffocating within it frees. Run. Get the fuck out. Save yourself.

Ariane whimpers and clutches her mother's ankles. Katrin feels her tummy clench, the shaky feeling of her wrists. Who was I? Who am I now? She looks around and sees her authorship in all of it. Still she can't believe she'd ever wanted this life, this fabric-softener-scented necrosis.

Asleep, Peter's breathing is a rustle of raw silk. Katrin gets out of bed, goes down to the basement, presses her palms into the computer's unyielding plastic.

Somebody has made a Room 221A Facebook page. Warbly, Ole Bill, most of the others are online. Nobody sleeps.

There's only one topic. They trade details like she once swapped hockey cards with her brothers.

Depressed mom.

World of Warcraft.

Bad case of acne.

Dead crows in the backyard.

Neighbours creeped out.

Got 'em. Got 'em, she thinks.

And then one day, this:

Picked the wrong room.

Sorry, what?

Yeah. Shooter buddy had the wrong room. Wanted to carve up the physics prof who failed him a year earlier.

Yeah. I heard that too. Choked on his own blood clutching this semester's schedule. But it was an early version, before the room changes.

Fuckin' guy planned everything but had the wrong fuckin' schedule. Ha!

Trade.

U ok?

It's not funny.

Hey, nobody died.

He died.

He deserved it.

The computer screen goes black, stays black.

Katrin walks at night. Her survey smells of ozone and unraked leaves. The reproduction street lamps hiss. She sheds the flagstones, the Kentucky Blue Grass, the cast iron urns of sedum for alleys of big box stores. They are silent places, lit up like landing strips in sodium yellow haze, whole tarmacs of emptied parking lots. She studies the late-season moths, pitching half-heartedly at pole-top haloes. She looks for clues. What makes a life worth living? Worth taking?

The few cars that slow beside her leave her unrattled. Men ask her to get in. Some shout out the things they need, the way they will use her. She keeps walking.

For an hour. Sometimes two. It goes on for weeks. Her body attenuates – strips down to a new leanness, searching for its truest form.

Peter talks to the college. *No, not yet. She's not ready.*
He calls her mother.
I'm worried.
He calls the doctor.
She's disappearing.

She walks in a new direction and passes a convenience store, and then she stops, alarmed. She recognizes the face behind the counter. It is Esam. Katrin sits on the parking lot curb and watches him among racks of chips and bags of milk, his stillness backlit by fluorescent lights.

She comes back again the next night, crouches outside the store.

She is in love. The untrembling mouth. The strength of his forearms. The genius of his belt pulled taut. The harsh exactness of him – they are the same person at the core. She can feel her heart beat again, her lungs push sorely against her ribs. She returns to Peter, before the alarm sounds, works her mouth over him like a cash-hungry addict. He wakes up crying. Katrin lies on her back, listens and thinks of Esam.

She walks to the convenience store every night. She feels desperate, stretched thin working up the courage to go in. She brushes her hair again, puts on lip gloss, fresh clothes. He is there, counting out change, stocking cigarettes. Katrin opens the door. Their lives are fused.

Esam is talking to another customer when she enters. Katrin flips through a few magazines and then selects one. She will buy something, respect the protocol of commerce. She stands in line and then there is no one else but her. And him.

"Hey, Miss. It's you."

She smiles.

"How are you?" she asks.

"Good. Good. Back at school, working a few shifts."

She waits.

"Hey, I visited Giovanna in the hospital. She can curl her fingers."

Katrin goes silent. She has forgotten about the girl; she has not gone to the hospital.

"Have you lost weight, Miss?"

She looks at herself.

"I guess."

"You look so different."

Now she sees what they don't share. He looks just the same, the very same as he did the first week of classes. And Katrin realizes all she knows of Esam is what he did. She doesn't know if he is originally from Iraq, or Palestine, Medicine Hat or Brampton. She has no idea how far his life has been pulled taut. How elastic he is.

"Are you okay, Miss?"

She comes to, nods her head.

"Can I ask you something?"

"Yeah, sure."

"What happened in the classroom, in our classroom . . ."

"Yeah?"

She clears her throat.

"That's not the worst thing to happen to you is it?"

His dark eyes retreat perceptibly. The smile flattens. He holds her gaze.

"Not even close, Miss."

———

The drive takes an hour. Katrin sits across from Giovanna and they do not speak. Her mother is in the kitchen making espresso. The girl shifts on the sofa, and her cardigan falls to reveal her bare upper arm. The bullet wound is a fleshy sinkhole rimmed with mother-of-pearl scarring. Katrin pulls her eyes away.

"Are you okay?" she asks weakly.

Giovanna sniffs and shoots back a hot, hard look. Katrin's face gets warm.

"What is it Giovanna?"

"Those stories – the newspaper stories."

"Yes?"

"Not one of them . . . Nobody interviewed said . . ."

"I never read them."

She feels the girl's centrifugal anxiety; how she grips the armrests of the chair. Katrin longs to flee.

"You *never* read them?"

"No. I couldn't . . . why?"

Giovanna pulls her shoulders back, thrusts her face forward.

"Nobody mentioned the memo. That you didn't read the fucking memo!"

Katrin starts. Giovanna's cheeks are pink, her eyes bright and glassy. The mother enters the room and places a tray on the coffee table.

Then the large woman kneels before Katrin, grabs her hands, and wraps them in her own.

"I want to say thank you. On behalf of my daughter and I, I want to thank you from the bottom of our hearts."

A tear streams down the woman's cheek and Katrin watches Giovanna stiffen behind her mother's genuflection.

Back in her car, she knows she won't go back to visit. Still she feels lighter, released. Giovanna's version of events feels familiar, akin to her own. She pulls into a roadside diner, orders gravy-smothered mashed potatoes and a butter tart. Her stomach throbs with its new fullness.

Katrin stops walking and starts sleeping. She sleeps at night and she sleeps into the morning. When she gets up in the afternoon she is still so dizzy with accumulated fatigue that making a bowl of soup leaves her drowsy all over again. She sleeps for a week like this, and then one morning she wakes to the sounds of her husband in the kitchen making breakfast for Ariane. She gets out of bed and goes down the stairs. Peter jumps when he sees her at the threshold. She walks over to Ariane, who is slouched in a chair, listening to her iPod and staring out the window. She kneels before her daughter, pulls out Ariane's earbuds, and lays her head on the girl's lap.

Finally, she awakens aching for her old routine. She opens cupboards, makes a list, goes grocery shopping. Between the baking supplies and confectionary of aisle 2, she stops her cart at the heels of a young man staring at her. It is Cody. His T-shirt hangs off him like a wet sweater.

"Miss."

Katrin smiles.

"How are you?"

He lifts a trembling hand to his jaw, as if to comfort an ache there. She sees his eyes are watering, the lazy eye more so. "Okay, I guess."

He hesitates. "I didn't . . ."

She reaches out and brushes his shoulder with her hand.

"You did. You stayed safe."

"But Warbly? Ole Bill? And the leotards, Miss. The fuckin' leotards."

His nose is running; he wipes it across his forearm.

"If I didn't, somebody else would have."

She pauses, finds something else. "Like you. Most definitely you."

She feels him deflate, right there between the Magic Baking Powder, coconut milk, and instant frosting tins. Weeks of something sour and uncomfortable escape through the invisible puncture made by her touch.

"I'm afraid all the time," he says.

The words feel extraordinary, weightless. They hang between them.

The air in Katrin's lungs thins. Her heartbeat whacks against her ears. For a terrible second, she is overwhelmed by the ferrous scent of blood, the crack of bullets and shattering glass, the taste of puke in her mouth.

A resin of sweat beads on her upper lip and she reaches out towards a kilogram of sugar, anything to keep her upright. It's the young man's arm that rescues her, provides the ballast.

"You okay, Miss?"

Her steadiness returns. She remembers now the glance that passed between them – a moment of emptiness, certainly, but something else, something warmer too. Recognition of the part of themselves reflected in the other, perhaps. She sees again how his body – the muscled trunk, the squat powerful

thighs – unclenched, crumpled, gave in to a bliss of forgetful-
ness, sinking into the shoulder of another startled being. Katrin
remembers, finally, how wholly the boy yielded in that
moment. The sight appeared devastating to her and, at the
same time, so very, very beautiful.

LYNNE KUTSUKAKE

MATING

Ever since his wife had planted the notion of Mitsuo's loneliness in his mind, Toshiyuki Nakai found that images of his grown son floated unbidden before his eyes with increasing frequency. These images came to him at odd times throughout the day, without any apparent reason or connection to what he was doing. He might be seated at his desk scanning the latest sales spreadsheet when he would suddenly picture Mitsuo trudging home to his dark, empty apartment. Or, in the middle of the weekly managers' meeting, when Yamakawa-san was reading the same monotonous business report he always did, Toshiyuki might close his eyes and see his son's head bowed over a bowl of instant noodles, which he ate in his blank, unadorned kitchen. Lately, while standing in the crowded Tokyo commuter train he took home every evening, Toshiyuki found he was repeatedly assailed by the image of Mitsuo lying in bed by himself, curled over on one side, his knees drawn up to his chin like a child.

But while Toshiyuki felt a growing heaviness in his heart

each time he thought about his son, tonight's event filled him with a not inconsiderable amount of dread.

He left the office as early as he could – at the last minute a colleague had wanted to go over some details for a new marketing plan, but Toshiyuki managed to beg off until the next day, explaining without elaboration that he had an important appointment and promising to take the document home to read. By the time he arrived at the Dai'ichi Hotel and made his way to the Azalea Room, where the seminar was being held, there was a long lineup. He groaned inwardly, recalling how anxious Yumiko had been. "Try to get there early if you can," she'd urged repeatedly this morning as she helped him on with his raincoat and handed him his briefcase. "Remember, this is for Mitsuo. We want to get good seats."

Toshiyuki joined the line, and immediately two middle-aged women came and stood behind him. They were talking in loud, excited voices, and one of them pressed up so close he could feel her warm breath on the back of his neck every time she laughed. As they had arranged, Yumiko was to wait for him inside.

The Azalea Room was spacious and brightly lit, large enough to hold a good-sized wedding reception, the function it usually served on weekends and holidays. Round tables covered with white linen filled the room, and in the middle of each table was a slender silver stand holding a numbered card. Over to the far right, at "no. 24," Toshiyuki saw Yumiko waving her arm at him. Normally his wife was not the type to flap her limbs with such abandon like an excited teenager, but these past few weeks Toshiyuki had noticed she was acting bolder and more direct, even at home.

"You made it just in time," Yumiko murmured in a low voice as he sat down next to her. "Here, let me pin your badge on."

He lowered his head in silent greeting to the couple sitting across the table and they bowed in return, their name badges – Mr. and Mrs. Yamaguchi – lightly grazing the top of the table as they bent forward. Through the doorway, Toshiyuki could see more and more people streaming into the room. The tables were filling up rapidly; it would be a big crowd tonight, a full house. The two women he'd seen in the lineup were on the opposite side of the room, yet even from here he could hear their loud laughter.

They were here because of something Yumiko had said one night several months ago just as they were about to go to sleep. "Lonely," she'd whispered hoarsely, following this with a heavy sigh. "So lonely."

At first Toshiyuki assumed she meant herself. Mitsuo was their only child and his decision to move to his own apartment almost two years before meant that the house was quieter than ever.

"It's normal to feel lonely," he said, trying his best to show sensitivity. "You need to get out of the house more."

"No, not me. I'm talking about Mitsuo."

"What do you mean?"

"Just what I said: Mitsuo's lonely."

"Did he tell you that?"

"No, of course not. Mitsuo doesn't want us to see his lone-liness, he's trying to protect us." Yumiko paused. "He needs someone."

"He's still got lots of time."

"Thirty-four is not young. But it's more than that."

In the darkness Yumiko shifted her weight and turned over on her side. Toshiyuki heard her sigh several times, the last time a long, noisy rush of air, almost as if she were trying to exhale all the disappointment she felt. After a moment, she said, "Do you really believe your son is happy?"

Toshiyuki didn't usually stop to think about things like happiness, but he definitely counted himself blessed in marriage and family. It had been an arranged marriage, nothing unusual for his generation, and it had worked out uncommonly well. Yumiko had been a good wife to him and a loving, tender mother to Mitsuo. Toshiyuki, in turn, felt comfortable in the belief that he was a solid provider. Even after so many years, he still enjoyed his job in the electronics firm where he had risen to a senior management position; he liked the invigorating stimulus of the workplace. Of course, work could also be subject to sudden shifts and unexpected changes – there'd been more than a few rocky times – but that was inevitable in the world of business. His marriage, on the other hand, had been a source of stability, like a thick heavy pole planted firmly in the water, against which he could measure the rise and fall of the tide, the tug of the waves left and right. Yes, marriage was a good thing. As a father, it was only natural to hope – to assume – that his son would eventually settle into a similar equilibrium.

After the lights in the Azalea Room dimmed and brightened three times in quick succession, the hum of conversation subsided and everyone watched a tall, trim woman enter from a side door and march towards the podium. The woman tapped her finger lightly on the microphone.

"Good evening, everyone, and welcome. My name is Aiko Mori, president and founder of Concerned Parents of Unmarried Offspring." The woman spoke in the crisp, confident manner of someone used to addressing large audiences. She wore a dark purple suit with a short fitted jacket that emphasized her narrow waist and slim hips, and her hair, which was cut very short, had a glossy sheen that reflected the light whenever she moved her head. Toshiyuki was reminded of the sleek head of a seal. "Tonight," Aiko Mori continued, "is an important beginning for you and for your children. Tonight is the beginning of a journey towards happiness."

A hush fell over the room, intensified by the dramatic pause in Aiko Mori's speech. Toshiyuki noticed several people nodding their heads. He stole a sideways glance at Yumiko, but she was facing straight ahead, perfectly still, her neck stretched forward as if pulled by an invisible wire.

"Happiness is a right," Aiko Mori continued, "a right enjoyed by every child, every human being. The bound duty of the good parent is to help your son or daughter find that path to happiness. All of you have taken the first step towards assuring their participation in the single most important passage of life: the transformative act of marriage."

Aiko Mori had a great deal to say about marriage, or what she preferred to call "life partnering." Many factors in contemporary society made it difficult for young people to engage successfully in "life partnering" on their own: the rise in the number of working women, the stagnant domestic economy, the high cost of living, increased sexual freedom, even changing dietary habits – all of these conditions were potential impediments.

Toshiyuki took the opportunity to look around the room more closely. Men were definitely in the minority here. He assumed that most of the men were accompanying their wives, like Mr. Yamaguchi, who was seated across from him, or like himself for that matter. One man a few tables over was staring blankly at the tablecloth in front of him and another had his eyes shut. But everyone else in the room – male and female – looked downright spellbound.

As soon as Aiko Mori stepped away from the microphone, a flock of attendants dressed in identical blue suits herded the participants into two groups: the "boys" and the "girls." The rules were simple. The parents of daughters were handed a pink paddle with a number in the middle, and told to seat themselves at the corresponding table. Their counterparts, clutching blue paddles, were given envelopes containing a list of their table assignments. Each visit was timed; when the chime rang they were to move to the next table on their list.

For several minutes the pink and blue paddles bobbed unsteadily as the participants jostled into place, bowing each time they nearly bumped into each other.

Toshiyuki followed Yumiko as she crossed the floor towards the first table on their list. Instead of her usual handbag, she was carrying a large brown leather bag that he had never seen before. They bowed to the woman seated alone at the table, Mrs. Sato, who rose halfway and nodded solemnly in return. She had an anxious expression on her face, as if she were about to be interviewed by the police.

After exchanging a few pleasantries, Yumiko produced a stiff document folder from her bag, and with businesslike briskness extracted the photographs of their son. She placed them on the table facing Mrs. Sato.

Toshiyuki had never seen the first photo. It was Mitsuo on an outing of some kind, maybe with his company. He was wearing a red plaid shirt and beige alpine hiking pants. His arms were folded casually across his breast, and he stood erect and tall in front of a signpost indicating fifty metres to the summit of Mount Hakuba. Mitsuo's normally pale face shone with an appealing mixture of health, satisfaction, and confidence. Behind him the faraway ridges of the Nagano mountains looked like the furry backs of large sleeping animals.

When, he wondered, had he last seen his son looking so happy and carefree?

"This is Mitsuo on a hiking trip," Yumiko began.

"Ahhh, hiking is a nice hobby, very healthy," said Mrs. Sato. She fanned herself rapidly with her pink paddle.

"Mitsuo has many hobbies," Yumiko continued. "Reading, for instance. American mystery novels are a big favourite of his. And going to the movies. He is especially fond of French films."

"Ahhh, foreign films."

"French films," Yumiko corrected emphatically, her mouth set in a tight smile.

Toshiyuki wondered how on earth she could feel so confident that Mitsuo went to French films. How did she know? Did Mitsuo call her up to discuss books and cinema? It struck Toshiyuki that, as adults, he and his son had never sat together in a movie theatre.

"What about Tomoko? What kind of hobbies does she have?"

"Tea." Mrs. Sato stopped fanning herself and drew her shoulders back smartly. "Of course, tea ceremony is more than just a hobby."

Mr. Sato, it seemed, had wisely decided to stay away this evening, and Toshiyuki couldn't help envying him. Although Yumiko had been insistent on Toshiyuki's participation, she was doing quite well on her own. She and Mrs. Sato talked for several more minutes before the chime rang signalling them to move to the next table.

"What a waste of time," Yumiko whispered into Toshiyuki's ear, tugging his jacket so he was forced to bend closer. "I wouldn't let that Tomoko within ten yards of our Mitsuo. Did you notice that one of her eyes is slightly smaller than the other? Shouldn't they screen participants better?"

At their next table they were greeted by a frail-looking elderly couple, Mr. and Mrs. Isozumi, who Toshiyuki at first thought were grandparents. No. They had come in the hopes of finding a husband for their daughter, who, despite a girlish pageboy and the best efforts of a professional photographer, looked old enough to be Mitsuo's aunt. To make matters worse, the poor thing had a prominent mole on the side of her right nostril. Without looking at Yumiko, Toshiyuki knew that she had her lips set in a "waste of time" grimace.

Over the next two hours they traveled from table to table, exchanging name cards and showcasing their son. Yumiko had quickly perfected her patter, introducing Mitsuo's vital statistics as smoothly as a saleswoman promoting a new line of kitchenware. Toshiyuki listened with not a little admiration. It was disappointing, however, that so few of the female candidates met with Yumiko's approval. Too old, too tall, too immature, too little education, too homely. While some of the other parents had expressed interest in Mitsuo as a potential son-in-law, Yumiko didn't like any of the daughters.

At ten o'clock they approached their final table, where an elegant woman wearing an expensive-looking burgundy jacket sat alone. She rose to greet them, bowing politely, and introduced herself as Mrs. Honda. Around her throat, she had tied a bright yellow scarf that accentuated the graceful curve of her long neck. Her smooth, unlined skin made it hard to believe she was old enough to have a grown daughter.

As soon as they took their seats, Mrs. Honda wasted no time in pushing the photographs of her daughter across the table. Keiko Honda smiled over and over in a series of large-format glossy prints that featured her in different poses and a variety of expensive fashion attire. She was a striking young woman with large brown eyes, deep dimples and high sculptured cheekbones. Toshiyuki noticed that Yumiko lingered over each photograph in a way she hadn't with any of the other candidates.

"I think everything you need to know is in Keiko's resume," Mrs. Honda said, pointing her finger to a sheet of paper encased in clear plastic that was displayed on the table. "I'd be happy to answer any questions."

"What a lovely girl," Yumiko began.

"Not at all," Mrs. Honda murmured modestly.

"I see she attended Keifu College. What did she study there?"

"English Literature mainly, but she also studied some French and German. Keiko really enjoys foreign languages."

"Mitsuo, too!" Yumiko's voice shot up a notch. "He likes American novels and French movies."

"My goodness, that sounds like Keiko!" Mrs. Honda's yellow scarf fluttered like large, soft petals. "She wrote her senior essay on Hemingway. And, of course, she loves anything French. Where did Mitsuo learn his French? In university?"

"He hasn't really studied it. Not formally."

"Keiko doesn't like formal study, either. We sent her to Paris for a summer when she was in college, and since then she's been back three times. She'll probably go again this summer. We enrolled her in French language school, but she tells me that most of her learning is outside the classroom. My husband grumbles that it's too expensive, but he can't refuse her."

"It sounds like she has a wonderful life."

"No, it's not wonderful. Not at all." Two little frown lines briefly marred Mrs. Honda's smooth brow. "She needs to settle down and have children. You can't go traipsing off to Europe your whole life."

Mrs. Honda reached across the table and picked up the formal shot of Mitsuo taken last New Year's in a professional studio. She held it at arm's length, studying it in silence, and then picked up the hiking picture and did the same. Toshiyuki was conscious that he was holding his breath, waiting anxiously for her assessment.

"A nice-looking young man," she said finally. "You say he likes France?"

"Oh, very much."

Toshiyuki glanced at Yumiko. Shouldn't they explain that Mitsuo had never actually been to France? He'd never been outside of Japan. But as if reading his mind, Yumiko refused to let him catch her eye. She focused her gaze intently at Mrs. Honda.

"Young people think nothing of travelling halfway around the globe," Mrs. Honda said, sighing softly. She continued to stare at Mitsuo's photograph, which she still held in her hands. "They're all spoiled, don't you think?"

"Oh." Yumiko looked bewildered.

"Spoiled and selfish. Just look at what we do for them, coming to events like this. Keiko is simply impossible. You have no idea what a terrible time I had getting her to pose for the photographer." Mrs. Honda paused. "What about Mitsuo? Did he cooperate?"

"Mitsuo? We haven't told him what we're doing."

There was a moment of silence before Mrs. Honda began laughing. She brought her hand up to cover her mouth. "He doesn't know!"

"No, I thought it might be upsetting." Yumiko stuck out her lower lip a fraction of an inch, a look Toshiyuki had often observed, a defensive pout she unconsciously assumed whenever she thought she was being attacked.

"That's certainly one way of handling things." Mrs. Honda laughed even harder. "I see you're the practical type."

Yumiko tensed her jaw.

"Well, I believe in being practical, too. I told myself I'd come tonight and gather as much data as I can. Aiko Mori has such a good reputation, I was very hopeful. But I must say," Mrs. Honda bent forward across the table and whispered, "quite frankly, some of the candidates here are a big disappointment. Given the fees being charged, I expected to find more doctors and lawyers, dentists even, you know, a higher class of candidates."

She suddenly turned to Toshiyuki. "Where did you say Mitsuo works?"

"Kita Chemical."

"You've heard of it, haven't you?" Yumiko said quickly.

"I'm not sure. The pharmaceutical company?"

"They mainly make agricultural applications," Toshiyuki explained.

"They're Japan's leading producer of fertilizer," Yumiko added. "With overseas offices throughout Asia and even one in Europe."

"Fertilizer." Mrs. Honda wrinkled her nose. "I see."

Yumiko began speaking faster. "Mitsuo has done very well. Salaries at Kita Chem are excellent, you know, with generous bonuses twice a year."

"No doubt." A faint smile rose on Mrs. Honda's lips. "I'm sure he's very good at what he does."

Around the room some of the other groups had started to break up and were getting ready to leave.

"Oh, it's time to go." Mrs. Honda gathered Keiko's photographs and slid them into her carrying case. "It's been nice meeting you. Good luck with Mitsuo."

Toshiyuki began doing the same, picking up the photographs of Mitsuo that lay scattered across the table. He turned to hand them to Yumiko to put in her bag, but she was glaring at Mrs. Honda.

"Such an attractive young woman!" Yumiko's voice was loud enough that several women nearby turned around. Mrs. Honda cocked her head slightly and gave Yumiko a puzzled look. Her lips were puckered as if she were uncertain whether she should smile or not.

"A beautiful girl! No, *gorgeous!*" Now Yumiko was shouting. At the surrounding tables all conversation had stopped and the room was suddenly very still. "But you can't help wondering what's wrong with her, can you? I mean, there must be *some* reason she isn't already married."

"What are you driving at?" Mrs. Honda's scarf had come undone, one end hanging untidily at the side of her neck.

"Nothing." Yumiko picked up her brown bag and headed straight for the exit, brushing past the two blue-suited assistants who were rushing towards their table.

They walked to the train station in silence. The wind was cold and Toshiyuki turned up his collar and dug his hands deep into his pockets. He glanced at Yumiko from time to time, but she gave no indication that she felt like talking or that she even noticed him looking at her. She had pulled her scarf up to cover her cheeks and mouth, so all he could see was half her face. Bending her head, she sliced into the wind with brisk, determined strides. The clicking of her heels on the cold pavement echoed inside his head, a steady tap tap tap that made his thoughts bounce like hard, loose beads. He considered what words of encouragement he should offer. The evening had not been good, but maybe they could sign up for another session or go to a different company. He thought about saying these things aloud to Yumiko, but decided in the end that silence was better.

As soon as they reached the entrance to the station, they were surrounded by people again. Toshiyuki slowed his pace as they headed for the ticket turnstiles, and reached into his pocket for his commuter pass. Yumiko would have to purchase a ticket. They stopped and faced each other.

"We shouldn't have come," Yumiko said quietly. She was looking past his shoulder, not at him.

"We can try again," he said.

"No," she repeated firmly. "We shouldn't have come. We should never have come." Then without waiting for a reply, she walked over to the automated ticket machine and took her place in a long line behind a young couple. The boy, who was tall and skinny, held his girlfriend in a tight embrace and every so often he would tickle her under the arms and make her giggle. "Stop it!" the girl said, squirming excitedly. Although the couple bumped into Yumiko several times, she didn't step back or even flinch. Toshiyuki could feel the stiffness in her short thick back.

As expected for this hour of the night, their commuter train was packed, and they had to stand for the first several stops before a seat finally opened up. Yumiko sat down and Toshiyuki stood in front of her, hanging on to the overhead strap with both hands. She closed her eyes and let her head hang forward heavily. Soon her body was swaying rhythmically to the steady motion of the train. Toshiyuki envied her. He didn't know if she was asleep or only pretending to sleep, but he admired her ability – her determination – to shut out the rest of the world.

The brown leather bag containing Mitsuo's photographs was on the floor under Yumiko's seat, tucked between her legs, held firmly upright by her muscular calves. Even at rest, it seemed to Toshiyuki, she protected the bag's contents.

He looked down at Yumiko's head, and located the whorl near the back of her crown, a slightly flattened spot the size of a small coin. Unlike the rest of her hair, which she dyed a uniform black, the short strands that spiralled out of this spot were grey, as if they had stubbornly refused to conform to her wishes. He felt an inexplicable tenderness for this secret spot, a sudden urge to protect it with the palm of his hand.

It was not easy to be a mother. Or a father.

For a brief period in high school, Mitsuo had scared them half to death. One day in the middle of term, during the crucial year leading up to the university entrance exams, he abruptly announced that he wasn't going to school anymore. There had been no hint of problems, of any particular difficulty or distress. His grades were less than stellar, it was true, but perfectly satisfactory nonetheless. If anything, Mitsuo struck them as better adjusted than he had been in middle school. But the situation quickly grew worse. He didn't want to see his friends, he didn't want to talk to anyone. Eventually he refused to come out of his room at all. Behind his locked bedroom door, he withdrew into a private world of music and computer games, inexplicably curling further and further inward like a snail retracting its soft, dark head.

As Mitsuo would not leave his room even to eat, Yumiko left his meals on a tray outside his bedroom door. In the morning she would find the tray in the same spot neatly piled with empty dishes and a "thank you" note written in Mitsuo's small cramped script, as impersonal as if he were addressing a maid. From the telltale signs he left, they knew he came out after they had gone to sleep. Toshiyuki imagined that in the stillness of night, Mitsuo roamed freely through their house like a ghost.

They suspected he was the victim of bullying at school. From the time he was small, Mitsuo had been a nervous boy, with a tentative, wide-eyed look, as if he was waiting for someone to poke him with a sharp pencil tip or stick a dead cockroach in his lunch box. In adolescence he'd grown into a tall, broad-shouldered young man, but that look in his eyes had never changed. His teachers, however, claimed they had witnessed nothing unusual. The district school psychologist was no help at all, merely reciting a litany of pat phrases: "hormones," "adolescent angst," "panic attacks," "fear of growing up."

No matter how late Toshiyuki returned home from the office, he would find Yumiko sound asleep at the kitchen table, her head cradled in her arms. He knew she was waiting not for him but for Mitsuo, hoping against hope to catch a glimpse of his shadow when he emerged after darkness. Afraid to disturb her, Toshiyuki sometimes stood for as long as twenty minutes staring at his wife, memorizing the curls of hair that fell forward over her arms, listening to her soft breathing. It was then that he noticed the whorl, the spot where her hair swirled like a tiny ferocious eddy. When Yumiko did wake up, he could tell by the dark shadows under her eyes and the long creases on her cheeks that she had cried herself to sleep. At those moments, though he knew it was wrong, his feelings about his son verged on hate.

"You never talk to your son." He heard Yumiko's reproachful voice. "That's why this happened."

Nonetheless it was his own voice that reverberated loudest in the dark chambers of his head, chastising him, chasing him down. You don't deserve to be a father. You don't deserve to be a husband. Not only was he unable to reach his son or comfort his wife, he didn't even know how not to be a stranger in his own house.

Almost ten months to the day, Mitsuo emerged from his room and began taking steps to reintegrate into the outside world. He lost that year, although in the long run repeating an extra year of high school probably helped him get accepted into Reimei University, a place that a few years earlier they had assumed was beyond his reach. Toshiyuki often wondered what had really happened during that brief, strained period, that interlude of utter unhappiness. What had happened to all of them? Mitsuo never talked about it, and Yumiko and Toshiyuki never asked. They couldn't ask. It was as if a heavy oak door had clicked firmly shut.

Toshiyuki felt sure that eventually Mitsuo would find his own way, just as he'd managed to pull himself out of his depression. Just as he had summoned the will to return to school and pick up his life where he had left off. It had taken courage, Toshiyuki knew that.

It wasn't easy to be a son.

When the seat beside Yumiko finally became free, Toshiyuki sat down.

"Are we there yet?" Yumiko's eyelids fluttered open sleepily.

"Almost. Two more stops."

With that she shut her eyes again.

Toshiyuki closed his eyes, too. The steady clickaty-clack of the train wheels over iron tracks, the long ride home. He recalled a night over thirty-five years ago when a much younger Yumiko had sat with her shoulder pressed against his, sound asleep. They had spent the whole Sunday at the zoo, standing in line for over two hours to get a glimpse of the newly arrived pandas, then racing off to see the lions, the giant gorillas, the hippos, the giraffes. They had wanted to see everything. By the end of the day they were dizzy with exhaustion, and on the train going home, Yumiko had fallen asleep instantly. At the time they had been married less than a month, and Toshiyuki, tired as he was, had been unable to sleep, feeling bound by duty to stay awake and watch over her. He had marvelled at the sight, the touch, of the young woman – his wife! – leaning against him. If only they could ride the train forever, he remembered thinking, shoulder to shoulder, the scent of Yumiko's hair filling his nostrils.

He felt a poke in his ribs. Their station was next. Yumiko had pulled the brown leather bag containing Mitsuo's pictures onto her lap and was sitting poised on the edge of her seat, ready to get up. She looked refreshed – her brief nap had done her good it seemed – and oddly expectant, like a schoolgirl clutching her book satchel. As soon as the train began to slow, Yumiko got up and stood at the doors. Over the PA system the conductor's nasal voice announced the name of their station.

Yumiko suddenly turned her head and gave Toshiyuki a quick, shy smile. It lasted only a second, then other people wanting to get off at the station crowded behind her. The train shuddered to a stop, a bell rang, and again the conductor's voice cut through the air.

Toshiyuki leapt to his feet and pressed his body through the crowd, like a swimmer pushing through surf towards the shore.

BEN LOF

WHEN IN THE FIELD
WITH HER AT HIS BACK

Almost a month before the button of a landmine depressed into its plastic disc beneath his boot near a river in Croatia, Sander waited in Munich for the connecting flight that would take him to the last assignment of his career. Back in Canada he was retiring far before his diplomat colleagues, comfortably they would say, due in part to a large life insurance payment from his wife's death two years prior. Lately he had felt rather out of step with himself, marvelling at his states of loneliness. How did I get here? he would think.

Sander was at the airport in Munich, trying to undermine the four-hour wait between flights. He bought his son a Bayern Munich soccer jersey from a boutique store, unable to remember if his only child still cared for the sport. He ate a giant pretzel as slowly as he could. After he washed his face and brushed his teeth for the second time, he went outside with his black duffle bag to the plaza between terminals, where dance music and an excited announcer drowned out the back and forth movement of travellers with luggage in tow. Next to the beer gardens, a beach volleyball court sat as if it had risen spontaneously through the concrete, its players – loud, strutting women and toothy, subdued men – uniformly muscled and nearly naked, punching and slapping the ball in the fifteen-degree weather. Sander imagined goosebumps like pox covering their bodies. A giant screen above showed player pictures and vital statistics as the announcer seemed to enthuse – from what Sander understood with a limited sense of German – about the greatness of every possible thing. At that moment his phone buzzed and it showed a message from his son, David: WHERE ON EARTH IS MY FATHER? ☺ A running joke between them. Despite his boredom, or because of it, Sander couldn't rouse himself into replying.

The announcement of his retirement had been received with businesslike approval from the Ministry. He was a minor diplomat, but lately he had managed to say the wrong thing at the wrong time, embarrassing the Ministry, government, and nation with astonishing economy – a few words, really – at two luncheons and a gala. An interview in Moscow had made small headlines, one where he went on about what he called the "death of diplomacy," ridiculing his government's efforts as "teeth-first" and "at times duplicitous" when dealing with nations in conflict. He would have been severely reassigned had he not stepped aside himself. It was made clear to him that this last job, Sarajevo, ought to be a trip without incident: simply exchange debriefings on positions with the opposing functionary, work the conferences, and bring back the new portfolio. "Opportunities for Canadian-Bosnian Economic Partnership" was the study, as remote from his mind as anything could be.

It was anyone's guess what to do once a career was over. There was maintaining David, but – perhaps when it mattered most now that the boy's mother was gone – Sander had lost the desire to tend to that particular connection between father and son. When David didn't come home for two days in July, Sander enjoyed the solace without too much worry, felt only stood up, as if by a friend. He hadn't noticed that David had already been disappearing with regularity. His thoughts were elsewhere, indistinguishable planets orbiting around a hazy cluster of dust instead of a sun.

Sander felt a chill and turned his jacket collar up, watching the airport volleyball with detachment, as if it was part of an unsettling dream. A jumping man cocked his arm and spiked the ball into the net, eliciting cheers. It was as if they had been playing since the beginning of time, and would spring, lunge, and yell forever.

In Eastern Croatia, the day Dragana saw a ghost, she had stopped at her husband's instead of going directly home. She was thinking of physical things: the sight of her students joyously pushing out of her classroom at the sound of the gymnasium's last bell. The chalk dust opening into the air like pollen of spent flowers as she cleaned the blackboard brushes. The muscle burn in her calves and her satchel, heavy with assignments, digging into her shoulder as she pedalled her bicycle towards her estranged husband's flat – their marriage apartment before the war over a decade earlier. She'd lived with her mother ever since.

Lately she had been dividing things into categories of physical and spiritual without knowing why, and this troubled her. There was a blind need to place things on one side or the other. The odd trip to mass with her mother was physical, the water, the wafer, crossing herself and occasionally beating her chest. Writing in her notebook at night was physical, the smell of the pages, the type of pen and pace of cursive and irrevocability of ink on paper. Coaxing her houseplants to grow, however, was spiritual, as was imagining a baby. She had been jumpy and irritated for days when she arrived at Krešo's door, which – unlike Krešo himself – would be labelled spiritual, as all points of passage were.

"Hey, love, you made it." Krešo smiled with his eyebrows raised as Dragana walked past him into the living room. He followed and lightly pinched her side. "You're getting solid – have you gained a few?" He grinned at her with his head tilted.

"Take off your shirt, won't you? I don't have much time," she said, producing a tin of ointment from her bag. He pulled his collar over his head and slid off the shirt before lying on his stomach on the sofa-bed. There was a half-finished puzzle of a spaceship launch on the coffee table, unfitted pieces of blue sky and cirrus clouds scattered to the edges and onto the floor. She straddled his waist with her knees and massaged the pungent jelly into the scar tissue on his broad back. She relished the strange, almost green light of the room, the remaining brightness of late afternoon filtering through the canopy lowered over the window, being in that familiar shade with a man she once fiercely loved.

Krešo grimaced as she prodded him. "They're reconstructing one of those office buildings, to think, after letting them be for so long." His tone stopped mocking wonder, softening. "Looks like work for me."

Dragana knew this to be a lie. He hadn't worked regularly in nearly fifteen years. "Krešo, you haven't a clue about building things. There you are reading a blueprint upside down and scratching your head."

"Well, what else? My life's as exciting as lumpy yoghurt." Krešo put his shirt back on as she took her earrings off in front of the mirror. She was forty-two but could have passed for ten years younger. She wanted to change before he could, she would get away from this city once and for all. They talked often of each moving somewhere else. Yet of course she would never leave. How stupid life was! Everything that seemed urgent one day would be forgotten the next. Krešo lifted her long black hair and kissed the back of her neck. Pigeons burbled away outside on the balcony. "By the way, I decided to humbly donate my talents to your cause, if you wish." Last week she had told him she wanted to risk it, have a baby – she was already well old for that. But her life without a child now appeared solitary, full of second guesses. She hadn't told him that a father hanging around wasn't in the picture she held in her mind. But this day she didn't want a baby either, just a quick lay. "Forget all that," she said flatly, rolling her eyes. "You're too generous."

They went back to the sofa bed and exercised their marriage rights in that dreamlike light, as if they were a functioning husband and wife. To Dragana this exercising was peppered with nostalgia, grief for an imagined existence they once almost had. When Krešo had come home injured and burnt just before the fall of Vukovar, Dragana was already at a place for refugees near Zagreb with her mother. Krešo then waited the war out with some relatives in Hungary, telling Dragana by letter that he was through with her. His wedding band had been blown off with part of his hand so he wouldn't be sending that back either. They had been married for just over a year. Dragana left her devastation alone during those months away, and when she returned to her town she acted the only way she saw fit. By then Krešo's comrades from the 89th battalion had returned too, but that didn't stop Dragana from telling her mother, stumbling into the kitchen drunk one afternoon – and by way of her mother the neighbourhood – that Krešo was missing and probably dead. When Krešo reappeared living and breathing six months later to stay, Dragana felt that she had tempted fate by lying about death when there were so many dead, her own father among them.

Now, once they finished on the sofa, she needed to go. It was Festival week and she had to help her mother get the house ready for a dinner. Krešo passed her a Kleenex from the coffee table and she wiped off her stomach. He quickly resumed work on the spaceship puzzle and sang a folk tune in loud falsetto, slapping his knee with his three-fingered hand: "Amer-ika, Amer-ika, don't go there unless you have to!"

At the bottom of the apartment stairs Dragana opened the door and then paused. She rifled her hands through roping, sweaty hair. A man carrying a black duffle bag walked on the road, about ten metres away, his feet making a faint crunch on the gravel. Dragana froze with her hands on her head and hairpin between her lips. Something was familiar about the man. After a moment she realized it was like a vision from her youth. Back in 1985, a Canadian boy she had been with for a few days, though she hadn't travelled to him in her mind for many years. But she must have been seeing things, for those years had barely touched him.

In the moment, the spectre had not registered her presence, looking straight forward, like celluloid film projected onto the street, a cut-out from another decade. It moved with purpose. A delivery truck pulled up and parked in front of the building, obscuring her view. She shook herself into motion and walked out onto the street. The spirit had disappeared, like it was never there; a man could not have vanished so quickly. She looked back to where it had come from. The train station stood silent at the head of the intersection down the way. Do ghosts travel by rail? She unlocked her bicycle from the lamppost and began to walk it home.

Sander woke up late in the new city and looked out of the hotel room window at the cloudy morning and street below. Three old men on the sidewalk talked with hands in their pockets. A young man entered an electronics store as cars meandered back and forth. Would Sander know her if he saw her? The day before, his assignment complete, he had boarded the return flight from Sarajevo, but at the stopover in Zagreb he didn't get back on the plane. It was early evening when he arrived in the small Slavonian city from Zagreb by train. He secured a hotel and found the woman's number in the book. In a cafe, he drank two beers and, with only minor confusion, understood that the waiter had never heard of the woman. Before sleeping he'd been satisfied with the progress made – her name in the directory was a promise that she still lived there after all – but as he stood at the dreary hotel window that morning, bewilderment flooded in and it staggered him. He tried to focus. It had been two weeks since he left Canada. He picked up the phone from the nightstand and called to update his son on his whereabouts. There was a long pause, familiar to both men. "You're supposed to be in Toronto tomorrow. I mean today," David warned, sleep still in his voice.

"You're right," Sander spoke softly. "But I need to, well, take care of some stuff."

"It's real early here, Dad. Four o'clock early. . . . Appreciate you calling but this probably could have waited. I've got things tomorrow. Today. Got university."

"It couldn't wait. It seemed like the thing to do, you know, let you know."

"Well, now you have," said David, collecting himself, sounding truly tired.

"I just popped up here, to Croatia. Sort of a whim, really."

"How long, Dad?"

"You can call me Sander if you want, like when you were younger. Angrier."

"Holy fuck. Happy? You never used to pull this nonsense." Sander heard an exasperated clicking. The connection, or the sound of a son whose mother has been dead for two years, he thought. It was true that the only reason Sander could put foot in front of foot in this other country was because of his wife's absolute and total absence. It was a nagging equation, but one that had bothered him less and less. He took a long breath, irritated, wondering why a child thinks a parent could be so incapable of change.

"Don't worry. Don't keep tabs on me, David. Just keep an eye on things there."

Air was audibly forced out of his son's nostrils in a long stream of disapproval. Or disappointment. "The phone's been ringing a lot. Your office keeps leaving messages."

Sander flipped channels on the hotel room television and waited for him to say something else. He came across an ad for a new hotel at a beach on the Adriatic. "If you need me back tomorrow," said Sander, distracted.

"What a colossal joke this is," David said, just warmly enough that Sander knew he was off the hook, that he could let the conversation drift into some dark corner in the back of his mind and not trouble it.

The next day Sander stumbled upon a piece of luck. He had woken early and set out walking the town for the second day, inquiring at various shops and kiosks on the surrounding streets, navigating concentric circles around his hotel. With no results, he resigned himself to go back to the hotel, stopping at a bakery on the way. "I know a Dragana Petrić," the woman behind the counter said in English. "She is a teacher at the gymnasium where my daughter goes." He got directions and bought pastry filled with a soft, mild cheese which he ate on a bench in the town square. He sat beneath the marble war memorial and silently sounded out the columns of the dead, noticing that one man shared the girl's – the woman's – last name. It started to rain, lightly. In his personal and professional life he'd grown sick of the slick meaninglessness of words, but a list of people who died on a monument held, at least, some sort of accuracy. There is nothing diplomatic about death, Sander thought, then groaned. He looked around the square. He once imagined the girl's home town to be a dusty, backward place, but only the prevalence of red-tiled roofs supported his clichéd guesswork. The facades of stores, café bars, and tenements could have been in any

European destination, and there seemed to be only a few con-
demned, half-skeletal buildings or empty lots of rubble left
over from the previous decade.

Later, mid-afternoon, Sander arrived at the gymnasium
and waited by the fence at the edge of the field in front,
hoping she would exit through the front doors. He felt a little
foolish, but didn't know how else to get to her. He'd already
tried both Petrić numbers from the book, in his prepared,
broken attempts at Croatian which relied on the pan-Slavic
basics of Russian. Both tries yielded quiet old women who
asked what, or said sorry, to his repeated forays of garbled
phrases and questions. The second one hung up.

He'd thought seriously about looking her up while in
Sarajevo, remembering that summer through his memory's
grainy lens. This was nearly twenty years earlier. He had
been abroad the last few months before he married; he prepared for his career and polished his Russian in Leningrad.
He then travelled southern Europe for a month. There was a
woman he spent the night with in Italy, another in Ljubljana
he fooled around with, and in Croatia there was another still,
Dragana, with whom he became entangled for ten days on
the Adriatic coast. When they met she had been holidaying
with friends and he was alone. They would walk around
talking half of the day and at night she would reappear at the
café bars with her friends to dance. He remembered being
with her at the beach, the sea clean and clear as glass, their
heads above its window pane, and their bodies wrapped
around each other below. The girl's expression seemed for a
moment so open and honest, excitable, before returning to a
perfected coy look that made him wonder if the alteration

had occurred at all. Had that really happened? Kissing her
huge eyes. They feverishly stripped and then tested the bare
surfaces of each other one afternoon in a room with curtains
drawn, then every night until he left. He'd said something
about the next summer. "You have been so great," she had
said before he left. After, there were two postcards sent each
way over the Atlantic during the next year – one he disposed
of before his new bride might see – and then nothing. Before
long came the nineties and the girl's country declared itself
and war broke out.

Now, as he watched the gymnasium doors and pondered
those final moments, he believed that there had been two of
him. One stayed there, on the brink, and saw the generosity
of what was possible. The other returned home and didn't
waver throughout the years as husband, didn't flinch as father.
Students began to emerge from the school, first a trickle,
then a crowd of dozens. None seemed to register his presence
as they made their way to the street. Then for two minutes
nobody came through the doors. The sun appeared, intense
for late September. He had begun to approach the school
when three young women came out. The one on the left
seemed to have Dragana's dark eyes, spaced wide apart – he
wondered if she could have remained so youthful. He realized
the impossibility of this as he stopped a few metres from them.
The other girls talked on cellphones; none of them took note
of him. He asked the unoccupied one in her language, "Does
it have in there, the teacher, Dragana Petrić?"

She turned her head. "Where are you from?" she answered
in English, her eyes holding him. When he replied she said
the teacher probably had left already. "I have to go." She

looked anxiously at her friends, who walked ahead and seemed to joke about the foreigner into their phones.

"But, the teacher, Miss Petrić," he said. "Do you know where I can find her?" She stopped, looking annoyed at his intrusion. But after a moment she sighed and produced a cellphone from her purse and called the operator, getting an address. He tried to appear good-natured, shrugging with his hands in pockets. She stared at him then, in that way that professes or pretends to know what was at the heart of the other. She yelled at the two girls to go on without her.

"I know where it is, it's not far from my house."

"You're sure she isn't at the school?" he tried again.

She shook her head. "You can follow if you want, I guess."

Sander introduced himself and held out his hand; she hesitated, then shook it. "Vesna."

They walked down the street, further from where he'd come, away from the city centre, past tenements in various states of disrepair and tiny old houses. She asked how long he was staying in the city. He didn't know. She looked up at him and politely smiled but didn't say anything else. "Is she your teacher?" he tried.

"She was, once. She is a good woman. All the students like her." Vesna was blushing and seemed self-conscious now that they were walking together, alone. They went on in silence for some time and then stopped at an old apartment building. The girl waited while he pressed the buzzer beside the teacher's name many times with no reply coming from the little speaker. "Nothing," she said. "What can you do?" Sander pulled out his cellphone and tried calling, looking up at the balconies of the top floor. Vesna looked at his feet, the slightly scuffed black boots. "Well, I live just further, on the edge of town," she said to him when he shook his head and put the phone back in his pocket. "Come have coffee with me and my father if you like, only a little while, and then you can come back and she'll be here." They started off again and quickly reached the end of a street where there were no more houses beyond and the road became gravel. Soon they were walking beside fallow fields. He suddenly had the notion she might be Dragana's daughter – it was unlikely but perhaps they merely didn't live together – her eyes were so distinct and similar to those he remembered. There was something older in them. They looked at him as if he was an equal, not a man probably three times her age.

"Do you like it here?" he asked as they approached a house on a large, fenced-in plot of land populated with plum trees.

"It's okay," she said. "Eventually I'll be in Zagreb, but for now this is fine."

The thought recklessly flickered in his mind that if she did in fact belong to Dragana and she was just the right age, well, she could be his too. "How old are you?"

"I'm nearly nineteen," she said as if it was a burden. "Older than my friends. My father didn't have me in school until after the war and I was eight. But before long I'll be finished at the gymnasium. I'm thinking about being a lawyer after."

He listened to their feet on the small stones beneath. "And your mother? This sounds stupid, but I thought maybe the teacher was your mother. And you were taking me home to her."

"I have no mother," she said matter-of-factly.

The house was very old but well-kept. Vesna directed Sander to sit down on a couch in the front room and then went into the kitchen. She returned with a sixtyish man, conversing rapidly with him, and Sander began to feel foolish for accepting her offer. He couldn't understand them but heard the man mention Dragana Petrić twice and nod his head. Vesna sat down beside Sander. "This is my father," she said. The man shook Sander's hand and smiled pleasantly. He went into the kitchen and reappeared with a plate of cookies and a tumbler of homemade plum brandy. From the bookshelf he retrieved a roughly sketched diagram on draft paper. It had lines and numbers on it, a misshapen house in the middle and a river at the bottom. He placed this on the coffee table directly in front of Sander. Vesna rolled her eyes and spoke harsh words at the man. "Don't pay him any attention," she said. "He's always trying to make some deal." He held up the piece of paper.

When he left over an hour later, Sander's face burned from the strong alcohol and a tint of anger, the piece of paper folded into his back pocket. The man had wanted to sell him the property directly next to them and the house on it for a total of twenty thousand euros. From what he understood, a Serbian family had rented there before the war and hadn't returned after. The price was cheap, but the land hadn't been officially cleared of mines yet. He thought it possible that the girl had taken him all that way to make a sales pitch – it seemed likely that they needed some money. Others had gone over the land and found nothing in the way of anti-personnel explosives, the man had said, forcing Vesna to translate. Eventually Sander began to suspect that the father was meaning to say Vesna would be more helpful with Dragana if he helped them with their money problems. Being a diplomat, the idea of blackmail normally put a wry grin on his face, but just then he felt foolish to be there. All that land would be his, the father had been saying in broken English. "Leave him alone," Vesna ordered her father. To keep him quiet she occupied Sander with many questions about Canada.

When he felt it was time to go, Sander thanked them for the hospitality and accepted the diagram, to pacify the man. "Dragana Petrić," the man had said again, by way of goodbye. "Yes, of course." Wishing him good luck, Vesna had put her hand on his shoulder just before he rose off the couch, and her eyes, and the idea of Dragana, held him again for a moment. Now, as he walked off of their property, another phone call to Dragana produced nothing. It was dark and he was getting nowhere. He kicked at the gravel as he turned onto the road.

The last day of the fall festival had been full of anticipation. Her small city hosted the huge week-long cultural festival every year, attracting people from all over the former Yugoslavia, as well as Italians, Germans, Hungarians, Czechs, and others. The last night featured the finale concert, and celebrations spilled out from the town square. Dragana waded through the crowds with her mother, who wanted to find Krešo at his volunteer security post and give him some baking. Dragana had brushed off the webbing of last night's dreams of ghosts that had clung to her most of the day. One ghost, that young man she thought she'd seen in front of Krešo's, doing card tricks on the beach in 1985. The determination in his brow when he taught her one, holding her wrists to show her hands what to do. Another spirit in a different dream, her father, spooning cascades of sugar into her tiny cupped hands. As if extracting from Dragana's unconscious, her mother had spoken earlier of her father's pension – as she often did – but also of a foreign man who'd telephoned yesterday, and she'd only understood that he was looking for Dragana. She thought her mother must be mistaken.

It was past midnight when they ran into her former student, Vesna, who insisted she show Dragana something, her eyes pleading. Dragana relented and left her mother talking with her uncle and followed the student's back through the surging crowd that had already filled the main square. A traditional Slavonian band with mandolins shared the stage with a rock group, playing ballads and lively anthems in succession. Dragana and Vesna approached the Gradska Kavana cafe on the edge of the square. Most of the tables had been taken away to make room, but one remaining held a man alone, smoking with his back to the wall. Vesna told her she had found him at the square and told him to wait a few minutes for her return. She had a way of gaining trust, making one feel on the inside of a conspiracy.

Dragana saw the man's head slightly bowed, completely disengaged from the festival. She'd never seen anything so solitary. As they got closer she saw that he had a kind face. His cellphone rang but he watched the two of them approach and silenced it without looking. His eyes widened as he rose from the table and made two awkward steps. "I didn't know . . . she was going to. . . ." He gestured at Vesna with a crooked finger before letting his hand drop.

Dragana realized then he was the same man as the one from the vision days earlier. She faltered as she was about to speak. Instead, she turned to the student, looking at the schemer suspiciously, and told her to run and tell her mother that she would be a few minutes. And then Vesna was gone.

In English, she asked him if he was in fact the Canadian she had known once. "I think I saw you walking the other day." The music was so loud that her words were barely audible to him. She opened her eyes wide to him and he laughed. He walked forward and raised his arms a little. Dragana reluctantly stepped in between them and let him hold her. She liked his smell, a freshness she associated with manliness. People began to dance in giant circling lines behind them, a snake uncoiling. They straightened out of the embrace and she asked him what he was doing back in Croatia.

"I was actually in Sarajevo on business, but then thought I would come find you."

"Oh," she said, trying to hide her unease.

"The name of your city has been kicking around my head ever since . . ." his voice trailed off.

She didn't quite understand what he meant. The music and crowd made it hard to capture everything said. At that moment she reluctantly said farewell to the ghost of him, that notion of an old spirit reviving an exact past. In its place was something unsettling, incomprehensible. This man had thought to seek her out.

"It's, well, such a surprise to see you. You haven't grown much older looking," she said.

"You neither," he interjected, smiling. "You haven't changed."

The absurdity and boldness of the statement struck her. She had in fact changed, irreversibly. That other person he presumed to know was a mere fraction of her self. "Maybe we can go somewhere quieter," she said, "so we can hear." As they walked down the first street, she was startled to see Krešo under the canopy of a crowded bar and wondered if he had seen her too.

A few blocks away, they found themselves walking along the river under the light of the moon, which was nearly full. A cluster of teenagers drank spirits on the bank opposite, and a young couple were beneath a tree further down.

"Do you have a family?" she asked.

"A son," he said.

"But you're not married?"

"I was. Are you?"

She wasn't sure which answer would be the most honest, which the best, and if those were the same thing. "I was. I mean, I once thought he was gone for good, but he lives here, in town, on Jelačić." She knew Sander couldn't possibly know street names.

"My wife had an aneurism and died quite suddenly."

"I'm sorry," she said, wondering if it was recent. "How terrible."

"No, I'm sorry." He shook his head. "I don't want to impose. Don't even know what I'm doing here."

She grabbed his hand to comfort him, but then felt disingenuous, and quickly dropped it. "How long will you stay?"

"Well, that depends. On things." He looked at her but she was focusing on something in the distance. They caught up on the generalities of life for the next few minutes as they walked. She had never been to Sarajevo so he told her about visiting the Tunnel of Hope, the city's only link to the outside world when it was under siege for three years in the nineties. He said that to get to it you had to go down into the basement of a house, that the original tunnel's 800 metres were dug entirely with a pick and a shovel. He also mentioned the assassination museum, precisely at the spot where Franz Ferdinand was shot. How he had stood for a long time in front of the museum's storyboards, pictures, and artefacts, the gun and the killer who pulled the trigger. How the pants the man – a boy really, no older than his own son – wore that day were encased in glass right in front of him.

At her suggestion, they started walking back the way they came. "And what about your son?" she asked. "Don't you worry about him?"

"He's a man now – what about him? Listen. I've been thinking about you so much the last week. Too much, probably. That summer on the coast." He kept slowing down and turning towards her, almost stopping. Each time she continued walking, looking straight ahead. "I want to reinvent myself." He seemed to be concentrating hard on the words.

"Hmm," she said, unsure. "Such high expectations!" She needed to lighten the conversation. "I really don't think that people invent themselves. Moments do, conflicts and catastrophes do. Other people do." She wondered how he thought he could have control over such things. The novelty of their reunion had begun to wear off.

"The diplomat in me might agree," he said. He stopped, clasping her elbow, but she kept moving so that he had no choice but to keep up. Back at the square, fireworks went off above them. He invited her to his hotel. He'd bought some wine that afternoon and they could drink it. She needed to get back though. And she couldn't very well bring Sander to her family and try to explain; she wasn't sure she wanted to. "They're expecting me. I don't know what to say. Another time."

He began to raise his hands, as if to embrace or run them along her cheeks, but instead stretched his arms above his head and made an exaggerated yawn. "Come to me tomorrow, will you?"

"Yes," she said. "It's a good idea." They agreed on a time, both smiled, and when they hugged she practically bounced off of him, and then hurried into the crowd.

The next day there was no knock on his hotel room door at the arranged time. Two hours had passed. When he called she answered and in a formal tone told him something had come up. She had to look after her mother and it was a bad time, many term-end papers to mark, but it was good to run into him after all these years and she hoped he was having a nice stay so far. She said it was a shame that he would have to leave soon. He tried sounding natural, saying, "Yes, we'll have to squeeze in a visit before then."

Dropping his cellphone onto the bed, following it with his body, Sander laid himself open to agony tempered by drink. Three litres of homemade wine were half gone by early evening. Everything was confused. He was on the other side of the world. The room was starting to fade in and out. He saw his wife's face. He saw Dragana. He wasn't one to go looking for punishment, but thinking about his wife he endured a sliver of guilt. She had moved out of the world never suspecting he strayed from her. In the bathroom he stripped naked and splashed his face, saying aloud, "Grief is a currency I refuse to deal in." He laughed at this, and then caught his toe on the doorframe, howling. He grimaced and hopped back to the bed. There was a sleight of hand, in a backroom somewhere: even the most natural, easiest bonds of intimacy would dissolve when one wasn't looking, and there would be no proof, ever, that they truly existed in the first place. It was stupid, dangerous, to go looking for them. He slept face down on the hotel room carpet.

The next morning, still drunk, toe throbbing, he heaved himself up and made it to the small table in the corner of the room. His whole being leaned on the table. His forehead rested on his forearm and his heart beat through his forehead and rocked his arm so that the table quivered slightly. His heart ran dry, sputtering. He thought he might die, but in the next moment there was a knocking, and it wasn't his heart. He limped over and peered through the peephole. When he opened the door, Vesna walked past him and sat on the edge of the bed. She shrugged happily as he stood staring at her. "I just asked for the foreigner's room."

At noon they were at the front edge of the abandoned property, one lot over from Vesna's house. It was raining again, and cold. Sander had looked Vesna's father in the eyes and shaken his hand. Minutes later he was on the phone, moving money around so that he could get at it with ease – he knew bankers everywhere. Twin curtains of black nothingness were slowly being drawn over everything Sander saw, spoke, heard. Yet, just looking at the property, he was already attached somehow to the wild-looking field and its empty little house. Vesna translated back and forth between the men. Sander wanted to know whether they had flails to clear fields in the region yet, the big chains that would circle through the soil and trigger anything still there, even the plastic-shell mines that many handheld metal detectors would miss. The UN teams used them. They also used special dogs. Vesna said that they had neither, too expensive, and without a tank the flails couldn't be operated anyway. But they did have an old handheld left temporarily at the property, part of some old equipment paid for by a philanthropic American couple through an adopt-a-minefield program. Vesna's father angrily emphasized that both lots had been checked thoroughly and nothing had been found. The rain lifted a bit. There was a yellow sign down the road with a red skull and crossbones on it that said NE PRILAZITE. Vesna's father handed Sander the keys to the old house.

It was a perfectly square structure consisting of a main room and two empty bedrooms on one side. At one end of the main room there was a couch. The other boasted a function-ing stove, a rusty sink, and orange-painted cupboards with one door missing to reveal three pots stacked inside, a packet of coffee, and a container of flour. Directly behind the cabin was an outhouse a few paces away.

Every redeeming particle of drunkenness worn off by then, Sander became immensely hungover. He dropped his duffle bag on the concrete in the middle of the room. Then he col-lapsed onto the couch and clouds of dust rose up on either side of him. He owned it now, all of it. The reckless prospect of the land was an unexpected gift, a quiet exuberance welling up somewhere inside him. He sent a text message to his son. THINKING OF YOU. LIVING HERE LIKE A KING AMONG MEN. OUR EMPIRE IS EVER EXPANDING. SEE YOU SOON. Within seconds the token response arrived, the phone playing its wistful little Chopin tune, pulling Sander out of his semi-conscious state on the couch. WHERE ON EARTH IS MY FATHER. DID HE FIND WHAT HE WAS LOOKING FOR? YOUR LOWLY SERVANT, PRINCE DAVID.

The following few days had their own logic, an internal rhythm that Sander didn't consider or combat. There were the mornings laid to waste, waking just before noon, shivering on the couch the first time, weighed down by comforters from Vesna after that. He called home every day but David didn't pick up and his cell was unreachable. Early afternoons Sander would walk to town for food, supplies. He also found a prod, trowel, and pair of helmets with visors. Mid-afternoons he would return for coffee at his new neighbours' place. He and Vesna's father conversed mostly by gestures and short words, and Sander picked up more Croatian phrases. The man winked at him now and then, as if they were in on something together. They played rummy twice, Sander winning both times. When Vesna arrived after school, she and Sander would don their helmets and prepare for the field. He carried the metal detector and she followed with the prod and trowel. At first he told her that her accompanying him was pointless and dangerous. But she had insisted on walking the field with him and her father didn't seem to mind. After the first time, they stopped wearing the heavy helmets.

Later in the week they had already covered two-thirds of his parcel of land. They were well behind the tiny house, making ground on the river. The hum of the detector often wavered into its high-pitched beeping as they paced across back and forth, single file from the last neon-pink flag they'd planted the day before. There were false alarms now and then: part of an old wheel, some nails. Any bit of metal in the ground would set it off.

It was nearly six o'clock and the sun was setting. Sander concentrated on the hum, guiding the rod in a small swath and then back before each step.

"I need one of your cigarettes when we're done," she said.

A slight wind picked up and Sander paused to look at the flat plains of Slavonia all around them. The rod kept humming, as if it was the current that powered the remaining light in the sky.

"Is your son good-looking?" she asked. "Sander."

He hadn't thought how close in age she was to David. "He is, I suppose. A handsome man already – still a boy sometimes, though."

"Will you have another one day?"

"Child? No." He chuckled at the odd questions she needed answered. "No more."

"I will have several when I am ready. Boys first, and after them maybe a girl. A girl I only want if she could have real talent as a ballerina."

This made him laugh too. "Was your mother beautiful?" he said. Then, more softly: "I bet she was."

"I don't remember but everyone says yes, she was. There are a few pictures." They kept on, doubling back over the next line up. When the wind wasn't in their ears, all that could be heard was the detector and the sound of their legs brushing through the overgrown grass – it was waist-high and higher in some places. Now and then Vesna gently bumped into him, barely, as if she hadn't been watching.

He looked forward to their quiet tours of duty, felt an unasked-for peace when in the field with her at his back. He was already preparing himself for the inevitability of reaching the river, which made a natural property line. He would have to render an excuse as to why they ought to start over again, that they ought to be certain. It needed to be safe and clear.

That night he sat on the couch reading a Croatian phrasebook by candlelight, making sure his note to Dragana was competent, if not flawless. It explained that he was still around, and asked if she might visit him. He would send it to school with Vesna in the morning after getting her to correct it.

A key turned in the door and Vesna walked in, veering a bit to one side, holding a guitar and a large plastic water bottle of red wine. "The old Serb from before hid keys all over the place," she said by way of explanation.

"You shouldn't be on the property in the dark," he said. "It's not safe. I thought you were an intruder."

"I am an intruder. And if it's not safe then I'll stay here," she said, plopping down beside him. "Until morning."

"You're drunk," he said. She passed him the wine and began strumming the guitar softly, momentarily shy again. She looked at him then and he saw that she was lucid.

"My father began celebrating with your money, so I took one of the party favours." She nodded at the wine. "I'm an intruder and a thief." She sang a mournful love ballad, her guitar playing smoother than her voice. Both stared straight ahead at the empty room, as if lulled. Sander tested the wine and it was good.

They drank for some time and she said how thankful she and her father were that he'd come along. It was a formal thing to say and silence followed it. "I brought a picture of my mother," she said.

"I want to see it," Sander said in her tongue, feeling the wine a bit, wanting to impress her. He didn't realize until she laughed that the particular phrasing had carnal connotations in the language. Vesna produced the small, round-edged photograph from her pocket and handed it to him. It was old and taken in partial shadow, but he saw that her mother was attractive, yet didn't possess the eyes of Vesna, nor whatever else made her so striking. The candle had wasted down to no higher than their toes. The guitar was on the floor. Vesna's hand was on Sander's chest, dragging her fingertips across it, and he haltingly lifted them to his lips.

"We should lie down together," she said. "If you like, I mean."

"Vesna, I don't think . . ." he said, straightening, trying to restrain the happiness the moment delivered. "I'd like to, of course. I would."

In that moment they saw that they could have whatever they wanted from each other. She took off her shirt, revealing a long stomach, high breasts with small nipples. He took off his, most of the hair on his chest gone grey. She stood up then and yanked his arm so that he rose up beside her. She was tall, almost his height. "I think we should pledge," she said, her eyes expectant.

"What?" He laughed, but she kept his gaze where it was.

"A pledge, like to a leader, or a country." She pulled his hand to her left breast, flattening it, and he felt the beating like tiny wings behind the flesh. She took a breath. "No matter how old or full of garbage or battered this Vesna-space becomes, it will keep a small place in it for Sander Torbensson."

He spread out her thin fingers left-centre on his chest and inhaled. "No matter how old, or full of garbage, or battered, this Sander-space becomes, it will keep a small place in it for Vesna Radić."

She led him back down to the couch. His lips parted the hair above her forehead, then kissed her nose, each of her eyes. The wind outside was rattling loose shingles on the roof, so that he looked upward as they tossed off the rest of their clothes. He was still in a state of disbelief at the turn of events, but in the same moment thrilled by a tingle of life re-forming itself, a feeling that was nothing short of hope. She made him slow down at one point, saying she wanted to enjoy this. She also wanted his hand gently on the back of her neck. And again her eyes looked at him, continually now, in that knowing way, like the very thing of him was uncovered with ease. She slid the cushions onto the floor where it was cooler and, starting over, he returned to her there.

Sander had given her a note to deliver and on the way to school Vesna – wanting him to herself, at least for now – briefly considered tearing the note to tiny pieces and letting the wind spread it in all directions, but she didn't. She knew what it said, had read it several times, knew it implored Dragana to meet with Sander again, as she handed it to the teacher that afternoon.

There had been suspicious talk of the foreigner in town for days, how he had taken land off of old Radić's hands, picked up where a Serb had left off on property that had been Croatian all along. "I'll keep an eye on that guy, that fucker if you want, won't let him near you," was Krešo's offering when Dragana had seen him the day before. There had been a flicker of the old Krešo in his face, for once drained of all posturing.

But Dragana was curious. She could understand the kind of man that would abandon his own life, but what kind left a son in the lurch she couldn't imagine. At any rate, she wanted to salvage something from her visitor, this Sander, something for herself.

On a whim she stopped at a clothing store she was riding past on the city's main street. She picked out a sweater for him, half-price on the sale rack, but it was all she could realistically spare. It seemed silly: the sweater was striped and had patterns and nonsense English phrases partially rubbed out in a fashionable way. It was the kind her students wore, but she thought it would fit Sander's long torso and he might like it, after all. With the sweater tucked into her satchel, she rode her bicycle on the stretch that would take her to the road past the edge of town.

On the way past one of the last city houses, two German shepherds lunged at her from behind a fence, barking with deafening ferocity. She swerved and her foot slipped and she almost fell off the bike, scraping her ankle on a pedal. She had always feared dogs, and it was a long moment before she realized they were in fact chained and unable to reach her. There was no blood. Recovering, she rode on while they continued barking as if they would tear their own throats out.

It was the first warm and sunny day in the entire week, and probably one of the last before winter. Dragana carefully pedalled on the gravel, yet felt more and more urgency to speed up and get to Sander the closer she got. The last few days, for some reason, she didn't feel as if she was merely tolerating her existence. She wasn't thinking of the physical and the spiritual. No, something was different, and if nothing else she wanted to tell this stranger her vague truth, that trying to reinvent oneself, though futile, must still mean something. She imagined sharing an awkward laugh with him, an understanding. Her period was late and she thought she might already be pregnant.

Vesna didn't come home that afternoon, but Sander wasn't worried, though he craved the very sight of her. He was out back by himself, carefully going over the last strip on the riverbank. He paused and wiped sweat off his forehead with his wrist. He turned the detector off for a minute, and without its hum he could only hear the river. He looked at the plum trees, all of them heavy with unpicked fruit, some of it rotten. Maybe he could bring David over and they could really clean the place up. The boy still hadn't returned his messages, and he thought for the first time that he wanted his son nearby more than anything.

Dragana spotted him from the road and walked her bicycle towards the river along the fence on the adjacent Radić property. When she was almost at the water and fifty yards to the side of him, she called his name. Sander was on his belly with the trowel, scraping at a rock beneath some loosened dirt. Looking up, he saw that it was her. He swallowed hard, but then smiled easily. He pushed up off the ground with a certain grace, like a man recently restored, and dusted his shirt with his palms. He then stepped sideways and walked towards her on the uncorrupted path, ground he had secured inch by inch.

ANDREW MacDONALD

EAT FIST!

The picture of Angelina Jolie in my locker stares at the Marilyn Monroe I've taped next to her. Angelina's lips are puckered half-moons ready to pull the tiny brown birthmark above Marilyn's mouth into their orbit. Whenever I close my locker, I worry I'm missing something celestial, a big bang of tongues and cheeks, hips and breasts. I look at Angelina's lips and feel their gravitational pull. Slamming the door, I whisper, "You want to be like them, not with them, Libby. Like them, not with them."

When I go to college next year, I want to major in math. I like the idea of isolating variables and breaking them down. When everything's a number, the world is a less frightening place. My lack of hips, for example, becomes just a matter of angles, of degrees or lack thereof, instead of the future C-section my mother predicts I'll need when I come into my "womanhood."

Whenever my parents ask where math is going to get me, I drop something on the floor. "That's math," I say ominously, pointing to the split apple. "And that." I point to the kid kicking a soccer ball down the street. "That's math. And look there." My finger follows a dragonfly that's somehow broken into the apartment. Actually, most of that stuff is physics, math's bastard child, but I don't tell them that and leave the room before they can ask me any questions.

For my mother, math is the solar-powered calculator that sits in a drawer underneath the microwave. Anything beyond its monochromatic keypad is someone else's business. Despite her innate hostility to numbers, she reduces my future into a single equation with the grace of a mathematician who's managed to disprove the existence of God: "No Ukrainian," she says bluntly, "no money."

"But I can speak it just fine."

"Think about your father. Tell me how he's supposed to read the letters you'll send us every month."

"Nobody writes letters anymore, Mom. Why can't I just call?"

"Your father likes reading letters. Besides, since you want to go as far away from us as you can, I can only imagine how expensive the long distance charges would be."

My father looks up from his newspaper, the special one he has imported from Ukraine, and shrugs. His expression confirms that things are out of his hands. Later he puts an arm around me and sighs. My shoulders are so narrow he can scratch his own chest when I'm in his grip.

I retreat back to my bedroom and stare at the *Tomb Raider* poster I have taped to the wall above my desk. "I want to be like you," I tell it as coldly as I can manage, "but not with you. *Capiche?*"

Angelina doesn't say anything back, but I know she knows that I know that somehow my hand has found its way into my pants again.

Ukrainians like doing things through word of mouth. Someone sees you purchasing boys underwear at the mall, to use an example that in no way relates to my life, and all of a sudden you're getting black lace panties and makeup kits for your birthday. All it takes is one of Mom's casual conversations with our dentist and the calls for potential tutors come rushing in.

From a list three pages long my mother chooses a woman named Alana, mostly for price and a little for convenience of location, since she lives three blocks away.

We arrive at Alana's apartment in all our finery: Mom in a floral skirt and a matching blouse she usually saves for church and job interviews, me in my school uniform – a pleated dress (shudder) and a loose-collared shirt that achieves the impossible by making it look like I actually have boobs. Mom sprays a cloud of perfume in the air and pushes me through it and into the apartment building's lobby. She presses a button on the electronic keypad and a muffled voice buzzes us into the building. Mom takes me by the shoulders and shakes me gently. "She used to be a teacher, Libanka," she says. "Grades I through 6." She picks a fluff of lint off my shoulder. "How's my makeup?"

She doesn't wait to hear the answer before making her way up to the second floor, navigating each stair nimbly, even though her heels are practically stilts. My heels are a fraction of the size and still my equilibrium's as fickle as a fish. After straightening her blouse and clearing her throat, Mom knocks on the door. Her fist barely touches the wood when it swings open.

Alana is a spectacle the way Godzilla is a spectacle. Her jeans cling to her thighs like plastic wrap stretched over a Buick. The shirt she's wearing is plain and white, loose at the stomach and pulling at the shoulder seams. Her extended hand is attached to a wrist thicker than a shampoo bottle.

"*Boje*," I mutter to myself.

"Very nice to meet you." Alana smiles as my mother shakes her hand.

"Pleased to make your acquaintance," my mother says in a firm Ukrainian I rarely hear. "This is my daughter Libanka."

"Libby," I correct her.

"Very nice to meet you, Libby," Alana says, her voice an echo. "Come in, please. I have coffee already made." Alana uses the same formal inflections as my mother. In English, Alana says, "Libby, if you want to make yourself at home, there's a TV in the living room."

"Go on, Libanka, while we talk *business*." My mother says "business" in English and when she does I know that no matter how colossal Alana is, when it comes to money, she'll crumble like the Berlin Wall.

As they engage in the great Ukrainian pastime of haggling to the cent, I stare at the mantel over the television, where a collection of trophies are arranged in rows like little soldiers. Golden figures stand on top of wooden bases, hoisting barbells high above their heads. They look like Alana: 3-D maps of bulges, bumps where I've never seen bumps, disproportionately thick thighs and angular chins. The inscriptions are all in Ukrainian.

Eventually I get bored and watch *Springer*. Two paternity tests and one crackhead intervention later, my mother claps her hands.

"Fifty dollars a month it is," she announces. She moves to the door. "Libanka will start next week." She gestures to me, patting her thigh as if I were some sort of pet. It shames me that I dutifully come as told. Alana leans against the wall and smiles, folding her veiny forearms across her chest.

The difficulty I have stuffing my feet back into my heels reminds me of the time my *babusya* called me into the change room at Zellers and asked me to help her squeeze a pair of stockings over ankles swollen to the size of tennis balls. Once my shoes are on, my mother smiles at Alana and pulls me out the door. We're halfway down the hallway when Alana's voice booms. "When you come, bring something in Ukrainian."

I stop. I don't have anything in Ukrainian.

"Don't worry," Mom waves, dragging me towards the elevator. "We have plenty of things she can bring."

At home, I'm handed a slim book, smudged with fingerprints. My mother holds it gingerly. "Taras Schevchenko," she says reverently. "He's my favourite poet. You and Alana can use him."

"You better be careful with that," Dad laughs. "Once I bent a corner and found myself almost divorced."

"Keep the jokes up and you still might," Mom says. "Treat him very carefully, Libanka. This book is older than you are."

The fact that my mother and the book of poems are on good enough terms to use personal pronouns makes me wonder what I've gotten myself into. When I read through

Taras, I start to get bored. He talks a lot about mountains. His words make me think of Alana.

The air in Alana's apartment is a strange yin-yang of smells: the steamy odour of boiled vegetables rubbing against the chemical-lemon scent of Pledge. There's some incense in there too, and hints of the perfume Alana was wearing the last time I was here. I'm sitting in a creaking couch and the cushions are swallowing me. As I fight their gravity, Alana deduces my level of comprehension. She says, "So you can speak, but not read or write?"

"I can read a little."

"Most people who haven't been formally educated in a language can only speak, so you're ahead of the game. Here, read this."

She takes my mother's collection of poetry off the coffee table and hands it to me. I struggle phonetically over the letters, aware that the words are poorly articulated, stressed when they should be a smooth river, soft when they should be boulders.

"Not bad," Alana says, "though Schevchenko wouldn't have been my first choice."

"Apparently my mom loves him."

"No offence to your mother, but she's wound a little tight. I can see why a stuffy old nationalist poet who writes about trees and fields and potatoes would appeal to her. Why don't we try something a little more fun. Here."

I expect a dense tome and instead get bright and colourful newsprint.

"They make these in Ukrainian?"

Alana claps me on the shoulder. It only stings a little.

"Wonder Woman comic books transcend the boundaries of geography and language. They're tough to find and most of the time I have to order them, but what the hell? If you can't read about women kicking ass in your own language, then you aren't really reading at all. Besides, the co-creator of DC Comics was a Ukrainian. Did you know that?"

"I had no idea."

"A Ukrainian also made Spiderman."

"You know a lot about comic books."

"I was a teacher. You're dead in the water if you can't relate to kids."

When I come home, my belly is filled with tea and *pompushki*, tasty little fruit-filled pastries that I wolfed down by the half dozen. My mind is a cross-pollinated jumble of Ukrainian and English words, fighting for elbow room with thoughts of Alana. Before I can even take off my shoes, Mom calls me over and asks me to write something.

"Anything," Mom says. "I don't care. Just show me that I'm not wasting my money."

I take a pen and scrawl the words Wonder Woman says whenever punishing evil-doers: "*Yisty kulak*."

Eat fist.

Sometimes I'm translating from English to Ukrainian, sometimes the other way around. Sometimes I spell things out phonetically or convert Ukrainian words, written using English letters, into Cyrillic. After that, we read together, alternating sentences. I notice that some words make Alana breathe more deeply, from the pit of her stomach instead of her lungs.

Whenever Wonder Woman says something clever before pouncing on villains, for example, she swallows gulps of air with the urgency of a diver about to break the water's surface.

The first few times, I make mistakes almost every word. By the third week I can usually get through two or three lines before running into an idiomatic phrase that makes no sense to me. The Ukrainian language refuses to flow from the page the way it does from my mouth. We go through comic books and magazines and newspapers and once even a menu from the only Ukrainian restaurant in town that delivers. The only thing we never touch is Mom's collection of poetry.

Today someone at school defaces my Angelina Jolie picture and rips Marilyn Monroe out of my locker. I find her pulpy corpse floating in the drinking fountain. What's left of her bobbing face slides off the page like a snake's second skin when I try to rescue her, leaving an inky black cloud in its wake.

When I get to Alana's, I stare at the trophies on her mantel and wish the gold figures would spring to life and crush my enemies. Alana brings in a tray of pastries and plops down next to me. Her hair is tied back in a ponytail and for the first time I notice how symmetrical her face is, her high cheekbones bookending a nose that curves slightly upwards, her face a perfect combination of straight lines and parabolas.

"You're quiet today," she says. She puts her arm around me, not behind my back but over my head, the crook of her elbow just touching my hair. Her breath is a wave of heat settling on my ears. I stop thinking about Marilyn. I stop thinking about anything, until I realize that Alana is looking at me, her head a planet tilting on its axis.

"Say something," she says. "Silence is boring."

I look down and clear my throat. "Did you know that if you put 23 people into a room together, 50 per cent of the time two of them will share a birthday?"

She cocks her eyebrow. "Really?"

I stare at her coffee table and notice three circular stains intersecting. "If you think about it, the number 3 is pretty important," I continue, building up steam. "The Holy Trinity, for example. Or how our planet is the third one in our solar system. And it's the minimum number of dimensions needed to describe a solid in math."

She looks at me vaguely and I sense I've gone too far.

"So . . ." I say, drawing out the word to buy me time. I consider talking about the paintings, but know nothing about art. The pastries look good but I haven't tried one yet. I look around the room frantically and find salvation in the collection of trophies. "What are those? I was looking at them earlier and couldn't figure out what sport they're for."

"The one with the red base is my city trophy. The big one is from the national championship," she says. "I set a national record for my body weight that time. Bench pressing twice my weight. Go to the gym and find me a man who could do that."

"I thought only guys worked out."

Alana laughs. "*Working out* is what frat boys do. This is weightlifting. Different thing altogether."

I've seen my cousins lifting weights before. Mike boxes and can lift 270 pounds off the ground. I look at Alana and wonder if her arms are bigger than his. She sits next to me and stuffs a pastry into her mouth. Flecks of powdered sugar float to my thighs like tiny angels before Alana's mighty hand sweeps them off.

"What do you do?" I ask. "Just lift the barbells over your head?"

"You've never seen a bench press? Don't they teach you that stuff in gym class?"

"When the guys worked out, we always played badminton."

Alana looks disgusted and for some reason I feel ashamed.

"I'll tell you what. Next time you come over, bring some shorts and sneakers. I'll give you a demonstration." She shakes her head. "It'll be a good break from all this reading crap."

Days later I do as told, arriving in shorts, a T-shirt, and running shoes that are still stiff from never being used. They squeak as I follow Alana down the sidewalk, toward the YMCA up the street.

I'm Alana's shadow when we move briskly to the change rooms. All around us, middle-aged women walk, breasts exposed, freckled, sagging, unashamed. I've never been in a health club and sheepishly turn away from everyone. Alana throws her gym bag next to me and peels off her shirt. She lifts up an arm and smells herself.

"*Oy boje*," she grunts. "I think I forgot to put on deodorant."

I tell her I can't smell anything. She peels off her bra and I can't help but look. Her breasts are like nothing I've ever seen before. They are small fists, pouches of flesh sitting atop two thick slabs of muscle. Her nipples are small and brown, the surrounding areola as vague as handprints on glass. As she bends over to tie her shoelaces, the slabs of muscle close like a vice. She catches me staring.

"They used to be bigger," she says, stretching a tight Lycra bra over her breasts. "But I'd rather have muscle than fat any day." She flexes her chest again, the striated muscle like outstretched fingers trying to touch.

The workout room is chaos, people in cut-off T-shirts and Nike sneakers moving from machine to machine like free radicals.

"Do you want me to watch?" I ask as Alana scouts out a bench by the mirror.

"Now where's the fun in that?"

"I've never lifted weights before, so I don't think I'm going to be any good."

Alana lifts my right arm and straightens it, squinting alongside my forearm the way someone trains the sights of a rifle. Her breath on my skin makes the tiny hairs I wish weren't there stand up on end.

"It's a shame," she concludes. "The distance between your chest and your arms is short and, judging from the length of your legs, it would take nothing for you to squat with your ass to the floor. Perfect dimensions for weightlifting."

"But I'm not even a hundred pounds."

Alana shakes her head. "It's about strength and weight, yeah, but it's also about physics. The less distance the weight has to travel, the easier the lift is. Like look at him. With those long arms, he'll never lift much more than 250 pounds."

I turn to look at a tall, skinny guy lying on a bench, lowering the weight quickly to his chest before slowly pressing it up.

"Imagine if his arms were a foot shorter, how much easier it would be."

"I guess."

"Go grab some weights and I'll teach you some things."

I wander away and pick up a pair of small dumbbells covered in pink plastic.

As I walk, my sneakers announce my awkwardness with every step. I sit on the bench while Alana lets her head fall from side to side, a small crunching sound accompanying every movement.

She looks down at me and sighs. "Leave those tiny pink things for the cardio bunnies." She pulls me to a crate filled with old metal weights rusting along the edges. "Use these. Now lie down on your back, holding the weights by your chest. Grab them in the middle."

I do as I'm told. Her hands close around my wrists and guide my movement. In a few minutes, tiny blobs of moisture start forming on my shirt. Alana kneels behind me and says, "Good. Slow. That's right." Her grip loosens as I get the hang of the movement, until only the undersides of her hands graze my skin.

I become a building Alana is constructing, each limb a brick shifted into place. The movements are awkward, nothing like Alana's fluid presses. Every time she moves to get a drink of water from the fountain, she leaves the bench glistening behind her.

"Before I tore my pecs, I was doing more than this," she laughs, kicking a dumbbell that weighs almost as much as I do. "The doctors said I was this close to ripping the muscle clean off the bone."

"Shouldn't you be taking it easy?"

She shakes her head. "This is taking it easy."

In the next hour, I learn how to spot a bench-presser and

how to bench-press myself. I learn about forced negatives, supersets, and how to use cheating principles for better results. I learn how to squat with a metal bar on my back and lift plates properly from the floor. When we're finished, my shirt is soaked. Alana has already taken hers off, piling 45-pound plates back onto steel racks in her sports bra. Some people are looking at us. Like Wonder Woman, Alana is impervious to stares.

The next day I'm sore, but in a good way that's impossible to explain. I poke at my arms, those broomstick-thick cylinders of flesh, feeling for muscle. I imagine that they're pregnant, not showing signs of new life just yet, but with the seeds of growth already planted. I shrug my shoulders, letting them lull back, the way Alana does before she does a bench press. I stare into the mirror, into my own eyes, until I become blurry. For a second, between blinks, I'm gigantic. I can lift cars and tear lampposts in half. Then I hold my eyes closed for a split second too long and I'm small again, a speck, a fraction.

It's raining. The droplets of water sound like Wonder Woman's high-heeled boots stamping against the balcony. Alana has asked me if there are any boys I like at school and the only response I can think of is laughter. "Most guys forget I'm even there. It's like, unless I have big tits and lips like Angelina Jolie, I'm invisible." I regret taking Angelina's name in vain but it's true.

Alana raises her arms and crunches her bicep with a wink. "Me, I'm too much woman for any man."

I am aware of how hot it is in her apartment, how much her arms are like something Michelangelo could've carved out of stone. We're sitting close again, in a configuration that's become natural: her with her arm around my shoulders, feet on the coffee table, me absorbed by her mass. She smells like perfume and sweat, like the gym and some kind of fruit I can't pin down.

I entertain the thought of resting my head on her shoulder but say instead, "Thanks for showing me how to work out. I mean, how to lift weights."

"You have potential, Libanka."

"I'd like to go again sometime."

I aim to rest my head on her shoulder but find her breast instead.

"Me too," she says in a voice that's probably as close as it can come to a whisper.

I'm visiting Aunt Olga for the first time in months. Olga is my mother's younger sister. She was only seven when she came to Canada, to Mom's thirteen. In Olga's cosmology, men are either chivalric knights or sleazy ogres. Women are either chaste or whores. It's a bright, bright sunshiny day or it's a deluge outside. Conceptually, Aunt Olga doesn't believe in middle ground.

I accept a glass of Coke. "Can you translate this into Ukrainian for me?"

Aunt Olga puts on her reading glasses, the thick ones she keeps hidden from the rest of the world. Her eyes follow her fingers, moving over each word on the piece of paper I've handed to her. She smiles.

"Who's the boy?" she asks.

I've come to her because she revels in taking part in conspiracies, hoarding forbidden knowledge, that kind of thing. She's our family's Eve, only she guards what she knows ruthlessly. To let the secret slip would be to ruin the power it gives her.

"Sorry?"

"There's no sense denying it, Libanka. You don't write love poems to nobody." She sucks on her cigarette and blows a stream of smoke over my head. "At least you've got the good sense to pick a Ukrainian."

Olga's boyfriend of two months – an American working in Canada for an advertising firm – recently broke up with her via email. History has shown that anything Aunt Olga touches wilts. Dead plants litter her apartment. Romance novels about chesty Victorian women and even chestier Victorian lords are strewn on the floor, their spines broken. Her cat, a mangy tabby, has yet to make an appearance during my visit, leading me to believe that it's either dead or has had the good sense to escape.

A part of me is afraid that Aunt Olga will screw the translation up. Another part of me concedes that there's really nobody else to ask.

She puts out her smoke in an ashtray the shape of Elvis's head and leans over the table. The tiny fissures in her makeup remind me of a Da Vinci fresco that's starting to crack. "So who is this boy?"

"You wouldn't know him."

"From the sounds of what you've got here, he sounds like quite the hunk. 'Arms like oak trees?' 'Lips thin as the ice I find myself on around you?' A bit sappy, but the thought's nice."

"Um."

"Don't be so embarrassed. You should have seen the crap I've written to men in my life. Feh."

"So you'll translate them for me?"

"Into Ukrainian? Sure, why not."

Her smile is the outstretched hand of a waitress waiting for a tip. I know the rules.

"Only, can you not tell anyone, Aunty?"

She winks. "It will be our little secret. Just promise me I'll be there first to meet him."

It's Saturday. I dipped into my father's beer and after one and a half cans I'm drunk enough to take Olga's translation and seal it in an envelope. I consider stamping the envelope's flap with a kiss but question my ability to put on lipstick. Slipping out of the apartment is easy. Dad's asleep on the couch, his reading glasses sitting low on his nose, a boxing match muted on the television. My mother's working on her memoirs in the bedroom, pecking ferociously at the typewriter Dad got her last Christmas. I wait in the lobby of Alana's building for twenty minutes before a pizza delivery boy gets buzzed in. I press my ear against Alana's door and pretend that the heart-beat I hear belongs to her. It sounds like someone's watching Jerry Springer. I can't bear to look down, so I drop the letter and use my foot to slide it under the door. When I step back I notice that the half sticking out on my side has the crescent imprint of my sneakers. I bend down and lick my finger, hoping to rub it off. I'm on my knees when the door opens. Her hand touches my shoulder. I stand and hold the letter out dumbly. She's wearing a housecoat, lime green, her hair a frizzy bouquet of blond helixes. She steps back and I step forward. When the door closes, I feel the chaos of atoms colliding.

—

We've started playing a new game. For every word or phrase I get right, she loses an article of clothing. Every time she stumps me, something of mine is stripped and cast off to the side.

She writes: "*Pes volossia*."

"That's easy. Dog hair."

Alana removes her shirt. "Fine, what about . . . *Raduha*?"

"Rainbow. You're going to have to try harder than that."

Off go her pants, her boxer briefs a glint of white between the tanned muscles of her thighs. "Okay, try this one: *Brodjachaja sobaka*."

"Dirty dog?"

"Vagrant dog, but very close." She points at my shirt and I strip it off.

"That's a weird term. Is it common?"

"No, not common." She stops, considering my body. "It's what my mother called me when I told her I was in love with a woman. She didn't know how to say lesbian so she just said that. It was the name of a gay bar in Kiev that was near our house."

The game stops after she says that. The pen she's been using runs out of ink. I kiss her mouth, my hands moving against arms, feeling her pulse through a vein that's like rope on her bicep.

That night, Mom asks me to write her something. Dad stands next to her. His newspaper from Ukraine is rolled up and tucked under his armpit, which means he means business.

"Go on, Libanka," he says, rubbing my shoulders as though I'm a pole vaulter or a boxer or a 10-pin bowling champion about to roll the ball. Shrugging him off, I ask what they want me to say.

"Anything," Mom says. "Whatever you spend all day doing."

Without meaning to, I flex my blooming abdominal muscles. They're armour and a cage at the same time. My hair is messy and I think I smell like the balm Alana rubs on her sore body after she works out, a pungent odour that I've grown to find sweet and inviting.

I take the pencil from Mom's hand.

In the moment where pen meets paper, Wonder Woman folds her arms and gets into her invisible jet and there's just me and Alana and the blank page in front of me.

I try to think of something like poetry.

Brodjachaja sobaka is the only thing that comes to mind.

ELIZA ROBERTSON

SHIP'S LOG

For my father, who once dug a hole to trap elephants

An accounting of the voyage of
HMCS Rupert
(Led by Captain Oscar Finch and
Navigating Officer Clementine Finch a.k.a. Nan)

Sailed: Monday, April 17, 1919
From: Sudbury, Ont.
Bound for: The Orient

Tuesday, April 18

1600

Light breeze from west. Temperature warm. Clear skies
except one cloud the exact shape of the birthmark on my
thigh, which looks like a bicycle wheel with spokes.

I'm knee-deep in a hole to China. Progress has slowed since
my Nan's noon inspection – must shovel for width now, as

well as depth. "China's a long drop," she said. "We'll want room to stretch our limbs."

1630

Went in for a glass of milk at quarter past the hour and Madame Dubois from No. 12 parked her Flivver over my hole. Progress further slowed. She's brought fruitcake and belated regrets re: Granddad.

Weather as above.

1633

I think Dubois's Flivver is a jabberwocky. (See *Through the Looking Glass and What Alice Found There*, page twenty-eight – "The Jabberwock with eyes of flame came whiffling through the tulgey wood and burbled as it came.")

1640

Dubois's fixing a pot of tea. Visit will be longer than hoped. Tried crawling underneath Jabberwock. Shovel wouldn't fit.

1650

In China, people walk upside down. That's why they wear those limpet-shell hats. The wide brims prevent the Chinese from falling out of the sky.

1654

In China, the sea is made from tea. During the third century, tea was so prized that neighbouring provinces boasted their wealth through triannual tea festivals where every member of every town paraded to the beach with masks and fireworks and dragon kites and offered their leaves to the waves in a celebrated public sacrifice. That's why each coast tastes different. Most of the South China Sea (near Hong Kong) tastes like jasmine, but the Gulf of Tonkin is rosehip, and the Bay of Bengal, chai. The East China Sea is primarily green (there are a few local variations), and the tides of the Yellow Sea ebb and flow peppermint. The Formosa Strait swells with a particularly strong brew of ginger root (Nan says Taiwan prevents open-ocean dilution.) The Chinese don't drink their seawater, though. It's too strongly steeped.

1700

Madame Du*bore* still here. She asked me why I haven't kept the roses hydrated. (The ones on the dining table, from the parish memorial.) "Un petty dry," she called them.

2100

Temperature: warm. Wind: not there. Sky: the colour of Granddad's toe after he sailed home from Panama last May to fight the German alphabet boats, which he never did in the end because they wanted him in the Pacific aboard an "armed merchantman," which is stupid because ships aren't men and they don't have arms and we're fighting the Germans not the Chinamen so why send my Granddad to Hong Kong?

Nan cut me a slice of fruitcake for dinner. She'd misplaced her own appetite again. John Cabot did not discover North America on fruitcake. I found a block of semi-sweet chocolate in the cupboard and ate that instead.

I miss Nan's old cooking. We haven't much in the cupboards now. Oats, farina, dried apricots, molasses, chestnut paste. We should arrive in Hong Kong within the week if I maintain shovel speed. (I reckon I average a foot an hour.)

I used to read with Granddad before bed. We're more than halfway through *The Narrative of Arthur Gordon Pym of Nantucket* and the *Jane Guy* has just been captured by the natives, but I won't finish without him. Maybe tomorrow I'll aim for two feet.

Wednesday, April 19

0715

Pleasant Mermaidian breeze from east. Some clouds.

Wanted to dig another foot before Nan got up. Found her in the living room on the arm of Granddad's button-back chair. She was leaning forward and her shadow made a falcon on the secretary and the fishbowl that sits on top of the secretary. The ribbon of her nightgown was untied and it dangled in the fishbowl, but I don't think she noticed. When she moved it glided across the surface like a Jesus bug.

I saw her breast. It was shaped like a triangle and hung over the pokey parts of her ribs. Then I noticed the slice of fruit-cake in her lap and the cashew clenched between her index finger and thumb and the dried cherry floating above the fishbowl gravel. I asked if she slept. "With the fishes." She laughed and her bones made a stepladder in her chest. I took the plate from her lap and said I'd feed Aquinas later. Made porridge like Granddad: simmer the oats in milk and vanilla until the oats plumpen and milk clings to each grain like melted wax. Nan declined a bowl. Left her with the swordtail.

1300

Dead calm. Sky like when Granddad made blueberry sherbet for the parish picnic on Dominion Day.

At the pit's deepest I've dug to my thigh. Starboard side needs work. My shovel's caused three worm casualties but I think they'll grow back. The soil's firmer now. Less like cookie crumbs, more like dough. Nan says it's clay. In China they bloom bowls and teacups instead of tulips and that's why we call it chinaware. There's broken pottery everywhere and in Szechwan province the lawns are mosaics. I'll bet Chinamen cobble shoes with ultra thick soles.

My own Oxfords are soiled with mud. Nan hasn't noticed. She's in the front, milking the crocuses.

1420

Found a live floater abreast the keel! He wears a scarlet tunic and bearskin hat – potential deserter from the Royal Guard? I conducted a proper interrogation, but he said very little. (He appears to be made of tin so I suspect his jaw is quite stiff.) I don't think he's a threat as he is little bigger than the palm of my hand – he will stay aboard as boatswain and I shall watch his behaviour. I went inside to introduce him to my navigating officer and found her in the bathroom applying white paint to her face, an emptied box of cornstarch on the toilet seat. Conversation as follows: "Nan?" "Captain Oscar." "What are you doing?" "Putting on my face." The plaster terrified her eyebrow stubs into fossils and when she smiled her forehead cracked. "But you already had a face." Her hand rose from the sink, which was filled with white gook, and she slapped her cheek. "Without makeup, I'd stand out in Hong Kong like a polkadot thumb." Her palm smeared circles and stretched loose flesh to her nose, to her eye, to her ear. She reached behind her head and her cheek drooped to the corner of her mouth. She didn't have enough hair to hold a bun and her fingers left sponge stamps on her scalp. I asked what I ought to wear and she suggested Granddad's uniform and I thought Granddad sailed for Hong Kong in his uniform but apparently that was the British one and he has a Canadian one too but they look almost identical. I went upstairs and found the uniform on Nan's bed. It's large but I reckon the waistband will hold if I wrap the belt around twice. The pants are funny. The bottom of each leg is wider than the thigh. The shirt's got a large collar and a blue and white–striped kerchief that I don't know how to tie because I was only in boy scouts for a year and Nan secured the knot at the beginning and I never untied it. My favourite's the cap. The tally reads "HMCS *Rainbow*," which is a silly name for a ship so I'll probably cross it out and write "Rupert." Nan's got a Navy photograph of Granddad on the dresser. I'm a spit image.

I'm hungry but the weather's fouling so I should return to deck. Winds blow fresh and there are dark clouds on the eastern horizon.

1800

In China, there's a pyramid of mandarin oranges on every corner. Because there are so many orchards, everyone helps themselves and the farmers replenish the pyramids each morning.

In China, they have dens where sages and scarlet women and gamblers and poets puff on the stems of poppies like pipes. Then they have extraordinary dreams, like none that you could ever imagine, and sometimes the dreams tell the future.

1830
Tried to make porridge for dinner but the milk wouldn't pour from the pitcher. Gave it a slosh and tried again. One drop dripped out the mouth and down the side of the jug. Lifted the lid and found a golden bulb lodged in the spout and six more goldenbulbs floating in yellowish liquid. Fished one out for inspection. Its skin felt like a waterlogged chicken thigh with a hundred spots where the feathers might have been. I squeezed and milk gushed through my fist, trickled down my sleeve into the crease of my elbow. Called for Nan. "Apricots," she said. "I'm necromancing the apricots."

Made porridge with water.

1900
Nan's face is paper maché and the whites of her eyes look yellow like she's been soaking apricots there too.

I think she's been in my room. Found a pile of white shavings on my pillow case.

2030
Monsoon! Brisk gale, downpour of rain. I worry my pit will cave.

2040
Tried standing over pit with umbrella. Proved terrifically dull.
Went back inside.

2045
There is a slice of fruitcake on a plate in the fishbowl.

2300
Tried to play Chicken Foot with Nan but she preferred to spell
words with the line of play. Had to find Granddad's Double 18
set so that she'd have enough tiles. He bought them on his first
sail to Bombay in 1892. They're ivory with ebony inset pips.

Nan's poems:
"Tick tick tick tick."
"Cherry tart, crispy heart."

My poems:
"Tongues clicking, licking."
"Mango meat. Yum."

This game would be easier if the tiles had letters instead of
dots.

Thursday, April 20

0800
Rains have ceased, clouds clearing. Light airs, temperature
like dishwater. Pit walls have maintained structure, but there

are two inches of mud at the bottom. Will commence drainage after breakfast.

0830

Breakfast: one quarter jar molasses plus two necromanced apricots. Painted a molasses moustache above my lip and Nan said I made a very fetching George the Fifth.

Told her that the hull flooded two inches and she said that was the size of my mother's tumour. I don't remember my mother well but Granddad said she was a dish, which means pretty.

1100

The boatswain and I drained the pit and dug another half foot. We're hip-deep stern to bow. It's harder to shovel, which means we're getting close. (We could be digging through a cement road in Hong Kong and we wouldn't even know.) Crew's complaining of thirst. Maybe the Navigating Officer will have lemonade inside.

1105

Nan's not in the house. The dining table roses are face down in the vase. Stems spike from the glass at 180 degrees and the water magnifies the heads into clown noses.

1109

She's not in the yard either.

1400

Scoured the coast. Found Nan in Mr. Arden's wood picking flowers from the riverbank. (Fortunately we've had a dry spring and this stretch of the stream is dry.) She says his April daylilies are the finest in all of Ontario. We gathered four baskets then lay between the stones in the riverbed and watched an eagle collect grass. Nan tried to string the lilies together stem by stem, but her rings kept sliding off her fingers and we could never remember where the clinkity-clink clinked from and they're coloured the same as the pebbles. So I did most of the stringing and my chain grew to two fathoms long. We wound it through her hair over her shoulder across her collar around her waist up her arm. She looked like *The Faerie Queene* by Edmund Spenser. I had to memorize Canto Thirteen last year for school. "Be bold, be bold, and everywhere, be bold."

1800

Light airs, some clouds, temperature cool.

I've promoted my boatswain to quartermaster. After writing my last entry we dug for four hours. The pit's to my shoulders now and if I bend my knees slightly it's as deep as my chin.

My shovel ripped a hole in Granddad's trousers. Nan wasn't mad. She helped me trim the pant legs to above my knees and now I trip less and my shovel speed has increased by at least a couple inches. We were sailing south at almost a foot and a half an hour, but we're inside now because I feel like someone is shovelling the inside of my stomach. In China they believe in karma which is like Galatians 6:7 "Whatsoever a man soweth that shall he also reap" and I wonder if I feel like this because I cut those worms in half?

Chinamen also believe in reincarnation. After death you come back to Earth as something else.

I hope I don't come back as a worm.

I hear shouting.

1804
Dubore's driven her Flivver into my pit.

I hath slain the Jabberwock.
(Oh frabjous day, callooh callay!)

1900
We had to stick Dubore's floor mat under the wheel and push from the front grate while Nan cranked the ignition and I fell in the mud twice.

She found Nan's appearance "startling" and threatened to call a nurse the moment she arrived at a telephone.

She wanted to take me home with her so I hid inside Granddad's chest, which is where I am now but with the lid open a crack so I can see.

The air in here itches.

1910
In China there are fields of garlic and rows of ginger and rivers of soy sauce and hills of peppercorns and plateaus of cumin and mountains of 5-Spice and clouds of star anise. And the grass is made from lemons.

Someone's on the stairs.

1920

Nan's gotten rid of Dubois. And she knows for certain that she does not own a telephone and does not like driving at night so she probably won't come again until morning, which gives us till then to get to Hong Kong.

2030

Dug to my nose. Pressed my ear to the ground and cross my heart I heard wind chimes. We're a few fathoms away, tops. Soon I'll be able to crack through to the other side, but I hear Chinese cement is extra strong. (It has to hold more feet because did you know there are a lot of people in the Orient?) Was extra careful around worms but it's hard on account of the dark. Nan called me in – said we were close, real close, and that we should enjoy our last evening in Sudbury. She wants me to help her look smart for our arrival. (Her flower chain has fallen off but the individual lilies are mostly unharmed.) I have to pack too, but Nan says we won't need to bring much. My stomach sounds like Mme. Dubois's Flivver. Might try to make semolina pudding from the farina in the cupboard.

2055

My pudding's erupted.

Details later.

2110

Left the farina and milk on the stove while I braided flowers into Nan's hair. This took longer than it should have because

A., I don't know how to braid, B., a clump of hair fell out of her skull each time I ran the comb through, which was C., gross, and D., hard to hide, but E., I had to hide it because Nan used to have hair down to the bottom of her spine, black as the ink in this fountain pen.

I maybe put in F., too much farina or G., too much milk and now H., it's vomiting.

Scraped what I could from the pot. It tastes like sand.

2230

We've boarded the ship, but Nan doesn't want me to continue digging just yet. I write by the light of our last candle because we are saving the lamp oil for navigation. I packed: my good breeches, a clean sweater, matches, Granddad's Double 18 domino set, his pocket watch, *The Narrative of Arthur Gordon Pym of Nantucket*, chestnut paste, this log, an extra pen. Nan's packed nothing, but she's dressed grand – silk tea gown plus the fox and mink furs that Granddad gave her after they got married and Granddad's mother's pearls. She's wearing both furs at the same time because she says it's "bloody Siberian" out here, which means cold. I collected the flowers that fell off her chain into two baskets this time and I'm going to try and fix a few to her hat.

I don't think it's how Chinese girls dress, but she says she feels like Queen Mary so I guess that's good?

We're going to play dominoes.

2345

Light airs. Temperature cool, clammish. Skies blacker than the bruise on my right knee, which I think I got from unmooring the Jabberwock. Didn't realize it was this bad until I started using my legs as a writing desk.

Nan and I engineered a domino track that winds over the whole deck, portside behind Nan's rear, then overtop the tin of chestnut paste to the bow where it figure-eights around my rucksack and me, then starboard to the stern, over *The Narrative of Arthur Gordon Pym of Nantucket*, and under the handle of one of the overturned baskets. We tried to make it climb the ship wall, but the tiles wouldn't stay vertical.

Nan wants me to pinch her cheeks to add colour because harlots wear rouge and ladies get proper blood flowing.

But she's still wearing cornstarch.

Friday, April 21

0015

I don't like pinching Nan. Her skin feels like butterfly wings. She dozed off so I stopped.

I guess I'll dig when she wakes.

0018

The air out here must be even blacker than my bruise. I don't like it.

0020

Nighttime sounds like this: hiss, chortle, shwoo-shwoo, crackle-crack-crackle-clickle.

The first three I attribute to the wind.

I've sent my quartermaster in a dinghy to investigate the last.

0021

Can foxes eat sea captains?

0022

I want to go inside but Nan's asleep.

Maybe she'll wake up if I light the lamp. We'll sleep in the house and I'll just get up extra early to finish digging.

0030

No luck. She's out cold. I even tried coughing extra loud. I'm out cold too. But awake.

Our domino track looks like the Great Wall of China.

Maybe it will defend our empire and keep out the enemies and we'll be safe as long as we stay within the tiles.

I just won't move, that's all. Just won't move.

0035

In China the girls bathe in milk and sleep in silk and walk in threes through gardens under parasols. The women wear chopsticks in their hair and fold the future into cookies. The men are warriors, calligraphers, alchemists. They make dragons from paper, fireflies from powder.

0040

I miss Granddad.

0045

Forgot the can opener for the chestnut paste.

Maybe if I read *Pym* aloud he'll hear me.

0515

I fell asleep under Nan's mink. My neck hurts and I feel like I spent the night in an oyster shell. Sun's below the horizon but I can see without the lamp. Hair's wet from dew or oyster spit. It's cold. I'm a bloody Siberian. There's very little wind. Dead calm.

Real ships can't sail without wind.

But this isn't a real ship with real sails so it doesn't even matter. It's a hole a stupid stupid stupid dirty hole.

Nan won't answer me. I didn't want to be rude and shake her so I made loud awake sounds instead – banged rocks on the chestnut tin, etc., but she's a heavy sleeper.

I want to go inside.

I'm scared my toes are blue.

I want to go inside.

0520
I wish he was here. I wish my Granddad was here. I wish he
was here. I wish he was here I wish he was here I wish he was
here I wish he was here I wish he was here I wish he was here
I wish he was here I wish he was here I wish he was here I wish
he was here I wish he was here I wish he was here I wish he

I hear burbling.

A whiffling in the tulgey wood.

Shook Nan, no reply.

It's coming.
The frumious Bandersnatch.
The jubjub bird.

The jaws that bite, the claws that catch me if I leave this hole
so I am hiding under Nan's fox. She's

My toe, my stupid stupid maybe-frozen-blue toe just knocked
over the Great Wall of China.

She's not answering.

I wish he was here I wish he was here I wish he was here I wish
he was here I wish he was here I wish

MIKE SPRY

FIVE POUNDS SHORT AND
APOLOGIES TO NELSON ALGREN

No one ever tells you not to fuck the monkey. Fuck with the monkey. Get fucked by the monkey. The monkey is filled with a selfish wrath, a vengeful will, a self-loathing so encompassing it eats at the fabric of others. And the preaching and questionable advice. The late nights and empty rooms. Bent over some bar, your face in a warm puddle of bile and ochre elixirs, the monkey with one paw on your head, the other angrily massaging your ego, your history. There was a moment there, not too long ago, long enough for affection, but close enough for regret, when the monkey was absent. But then came February. Bitter, twisted, poor self-esteem-ridden February, with its aborted twenty-eight-day life and that Hallmark holiday tossed into the middle for good measure. Like memory and monkeys, I've never trusted February, never will.

I've lost before. I'm good at it. Kids dream of gold medals and first place. I fantasized about fourth place, and certificates of participation. And at the time, the time without the monkey,

I was happy in fourth, even had kind afternoons when third felt possible. But then Dad died. Dad had once told me that love lasts about ten minutes, and if you're lucky you're not wearing pants for the second five. There's something humbling in my memories of my father. Memories riddled in prophecy. And January got shorter, and shorter. And my right upper back started to miss its inhabitant. And before I could find community centre basements, cold coffee, and familiar strangers, I found what I knew, my past. I turned to the monkey.

I got my 30-pound monkey when I was about sixteen. I'd like to say that I ordered him from an ad in the back of a comic book, because I'm old enough to remember when you could order exotic items like 30-pound monkeys from ads in the backs of comic books. Part of a simpler life. At least then I could blame Marvel or DC instead of myself. I wonder if you can still order stuff from the backs of comic books. I don't read them anymore, of course, so I wouldn't know. I still wonder though. But him? I got the 30-pound monkey from a scratch-and-win ticket in a case of 50. Stubbies. Because I'm old enough to remember stubbies. First prize was a hot tub. Second prize was a 30-pound monkey. Third prize was a Hyundai Sonata. I wonder if the other winners have had as many problems with their prizes. I wonder if they still have them. The hot tub I can see, the Hyundai not so much.

When I was younger, I would just play with my 30-pound monkey on weekends. My friends seemed to like me more with the 30-pound monkey around. Even the hot girls, the untouchables, suddenly began to pay some attention. I give the 30-pound monkey all the credit for my first blow job. Jill

Henley. After that I began to take my 30-pound monkey everywhere. Made me wonder about how he had filled his time without me. Maybe swimming lessons, because all of a sudden one day he could backstroke like nobody's business. But I think he just waited for me, patience being a virtue of the monkey.

Friends said I looked better with the monkey around, better groomed. I explained that I had to be clean-shaven around my 30-pound monkey; a full beard reminded him of a difficult past, of his father. He didn't like to talk about it. Man, did he get me laid during university, that 30-pound monkey did. For four years I was the charming, suave, confident, mysterious guy with the 30-pound monkey on his back. I was all the things I'm not, all the shit I'll never be. The girls loved it. He never seemed to want anything in return. He was selfless, seemed to live for my wants and needs alone.

And then we were supposed to part ways and journey into adulthood and careers and promise. The weeks were filled with cubicle nightmares and simian dreams. Everybody disappeared into their lives, faded into the background, tucked in their shirts, cut their hair and said goodbye. I guess we grew up. Or they grew up. Me and my 30-pound monkey had no such intentions. We resisted the temptations of cellphone leashes and bleeding ulcers, talk of divorce and golf. This was a new world, where a man and his 30-pound monkey were no longer kings, but rather unwanted fools. How does it happen? How does it change? You try to be a fucking adult with a 30-pound monkey whispering, We don't need these people; we don't need anyone, in your goddamn ear all night. You end up alone, that's what fucking happens, at some bar at the end of the night arguing the merits of Darwinism in an empty room. There's nothing sadder than an old man and his 30-pound monkey slurring their way through evolution at the end of the bar. It's how we end up here.

I started relishing that time alone, the solitude, the distance. Fuck people, we'd say and stay in and drink two-fours of 50 (just for nostalgia's sake) and watch *Every Which Way but Loose* on DVD. I bought him the *B.J. and the Bear* box set but he found it offensive. Not as a simian, but apparently there's something about Greg Evigan that really pisses him off. I could always cheer him up by reading him H.A. Rey's biography, or watching Terry Gilliam movies. For a while this life was good. For a while I thought I was happy, rid of those who failed to see the beauty of a clean-shaven man and his 30-pound monkey.

You don't really notice when it turns. I'd like to think I could look back and pinpoint an exact moment, but I can't. We stopped watching movies, stopped trying to find work. We'd just sit around and drink, masturbate, and argue. There was no happiness in this life, just anger, resentment. I couldn't get my 30-pound monkey to wear pants anymore. "Put on a goddamn pair of slacks," I'd scream at him through a hazy, thick, depressing room. But he'd just carry on pantsless, make fun of me for using the word *slacks*. Nothing wrong with saying *slacks*. I'm old enough to remember when people actually said *slacks*. Maybe they say *trousers* now. I would still say *slacks*, though, but damn if I could get my 30-pound monkey in a pair. Oddly enough, he'd wear panties. Loved panties. Anything with lace or frills. Only problem is he would tend to nibble at their edges, so while he would wear panties, he'd usually eat his way out of them within an hour. So I'd find myself at LaSenza Girl every other weekend, restocking his supply. I think the staff started to be suspicious of my buying patterns. One day I noticed them snickering behind the counter, and I wasn't in a particularly good mood – the 30-pound monkey and I had been up railing codeine and drinking gin 'til our eyes bled, so the sight of these whored-up mall workers laughing at me sent me into a rage and I started throwing all the panties and bras I could get my hands on at them and screaming, "You don't get it, girls, I've got a half-naked 30-pound monkey at home." Fuck them, fuck mall security, and fuck community service.

That was the bottom, I'd have to assume, from what I can remember. At that point I was drowning in the dregs. The 30-pound monkey, of course, was fine, gracefully backstroking along the surface. This was when I met Sara. Sara is my wife. Was my wife. I had seen her from across the bar one night. I was filled with the monkey's confidence. I told her, "I have no money and very little promise. But one day I'd like to buy you a house." We shared the rest of my cigarette and were married four months later. The church was Unitarian and her mother never showed. Sara painted sometimes. I wrote country songs about her in the garage after she'd gone to sleep. She was an insomniac, but she hadn't told me. She liked the secret. I guess I found out at some point. We would have liked to have one day owned a dog, and named it Oldham after her late father. I never met her father. Neither had she, but sometimes she said she imagined him. Slowly, she convinced me I could do without the 30-pound monkey. Oh, he fought a good fight, even threw on jogging pants on occasion and a Baby Gap

T-shirt, stopped putting out cigarettes in my hair and whispering devious things I could do to Sara while she slept. But Sara won out, and the 30-pound monkey crawled begrudgingly off my back, packed his bits of panties and an autographed Mickey Dolenz eight-by-ten and left.

Or maybe he never left. Maybe he was just hiding in the closet, chewing on Sara's underwear and waiting for an opportunity to return. Some nights I would wake up screaming about panties and monkeys and Clint Eastwood. Sara would ease me back into sleep with her soft, caressing hands and whispers of better days. Sometimes I'd find myself at the liquor store, looking for him in the sweet caramel diamond reflections of competing Scotch bottles. Sometimes I'd walk by a bar that struck me with some odd degree of familiarity, and I'd hear a laughter I'd think was mine coming from inside. Sara would pull me past, take me to safer places, without laughter and without my 30-pound monkey. Maybe she got tired of playing that role, mothering a grown man, of feeling second place to an absent 30-pound monkey whose friendship she could never live up to. Maybe I forced her away, making it easier for me to find the monkey again. Maybe it's the monkey I love, because his pants are always off, and that's true love, isn't it?

So she left. She said, "I deserve to make mistakes too. But one day I'd like to make up for them." We divided the cutlery, and she moved into a loft two neighbourhoods over. I stayed in the apartment and thought about moving and changing and dogs and things of that nature, but mostly I feared the monkey. I took to sedatives and a youngish waitress from the local. The monkey was somewhere close, always somewhere close. I had taken to long walks, and often asked for rain. I rarely went to work, and the apartment likely needed to be painted. The monkey called and offered to help. He came over, but instead of colour palettes brought beer. We fell down to some bar we had never been to, settled into bourbon and old habits, tried to kill Sara's memory. But even bourbon can't kill, it can only bring you closer to him, or closer to here.

Which brings us back to February, hollow chocolate hearts, three suspiciously missing days, and bowls of Scotch for breakfast. And Dad's gone. And Sara's gone. And I'm sitting in my emptied, unpainted living room with a bottle or two or three or ten and the 30-pound monkey is in my bedroom unpacking his things and I'm thinking can it really be this easy, to give in, to give up, to go back? But I keep drinking and the 30-pound monkey is mounting his Curious George poster over the spot where Sara's stereo used to be, and I keep emptying bottle after bottle as he wanders around whistling "Daydream Believer" and some song whose title eludes me but goes, "Come on come on, come on come on, come on is such a joy, come on is such a joy, come on let's take it easy, come on let's take it easy, take it easy take it easy," and occasionally dropping off a pill or two and maybe a shot on the coffee table with a wry and twisted smile, and I'm only too unhappy to oblige and all of a sudden it feels as if I've gone back in time, and that Sara never existed and Dad never died and everyone was without pants and Jill Henley thinks I'm cool and her mouth is warm and new and there's a contest to life and I'm winning and there's laughter in every room and it's there because of me, but in a flash that is brilliant and humbling and horrible and maddening and wonderful and spiteful and humiliating and festively blinding, I'm brought back to a room I hate, where I have no control, where I'm led around by a 30-pound monkey who has deceived me into believing he loves or cares or helps and does not hurt, or hate, or kill slowly, painfully, and decidedly like he killed my dad, like he killed my twenties, like he killed this room, this life, and suddenly I feel a power I've never had and a hate I never noticed and I grab a bottle off the table and I smash it, which gets the 30-pound monkey's attention all right, and I start chasing him around the room, and he's screaming and I'm screaming, and he's swinging from chandeliers that likely only exist in my mind and I finally get a hold of him and he looks up at me with evil piercing eyes and I take one deep, horrible last breath and I start swinging the broken bottle and blood is spurting everywhere, and bits of lace are flying about and I'm covered in his blood and my blood, and somewhere there is yelling and bellowing infinite sirens and bright lights and humorous lies and hungry mistakes and a simple redemption and an unsatisfying yet predictable end. And then I'm here. And I see the monkey in all of your eyes, and in the reflection of your knowing.

DAMIAN TARNOPOLSKY

LAUD WE THE GODS

I am a man with a secret. It fires up under my ribs as I push my cart along. I am a man with a knife under his coat; I smile like a bachelor tripping down his latest conquest's steps. If the boys of the neighbourhood (the rough shells, the scamps) do not trouble me now – frying bigger fish – it is because they do not know me; not as a man with a secret.

Sometimes it snows and my wheels gum up; then the metal of my cart's handle is colder to the touch than a nun forgotten in a snow-drift. I push my way along as best I can, my worldly possessions always in sight. My blue blanket and my bowl. Pushing this cart up and over small mountains of rubble, broken down wooden fencing that once upon a time were trees.

The boy said he'd found something I had better see. The others have jowly, sulphurous skin; but my boy is dainty amongst the banana peels and bomb craters. A slim hard face, and he fingered his knife as he spoke; the grip was decorated with ivory pictures of fox skulls. And yet he is a boy; they used to fall over their Latin pronunciation, their -*ibus* and -*imus*. He led me onwards; I wondered if there were more boys, more boys watching us from the broken windows across the way, pointing rifles.

When I was a priest, a million years ago, I was respected. The Gods are all in hiding now but I remember their faces. I remember the God with the drooping moustache, and the God of staying in bed. I am the one man in the world who knows them. Times have moved on, as our editorialists are fond of saying. I push my cart along and I keep the Gods with me: the sad-faced God and the God of building canoes. I stop to pick up pieces of postering; I pull chewing gum from my beard, when the mood strikes me. The boys in the neighbourhood throw boulders and pebbles and curse me, and I pray reverently to the God of knowing my own mind.

First there was a bank. I wasn't happy leaving my cart outside, and I left it and walked back to it and left it and walked back to it; but he locked it up with the chain he kept around his waist. If anyone wanted to take it they would have to carry it. Good enough, he said. The bank was a dusty wooden vault with green shades over tellers' lamps. Every teller's window was shattered but they had left the shades, I don't know why. Smoke had darkened the blinds long ago, it was terribly cold. I could imagine sportswriters working there; I mumbled something to the God of hair. I saw the body of a rat; are we supposed to hate baby rats also? I wondered where the bankers used to take their lunches, naturally. Not the proles with their brown bread sandwiches, but the executives, the captains of industry. They built a tower over the branch; but the boy said he wanted to show me something different. If you were my charge, I said, I would have kept you far hence; this is a treacherous place. His eyelashes were wet little ballerinas. I had a secret hope, of course. We all have our secret hopes, to keep us insane; just when we think we are starting to turn blue they pull us back into the magenta once more. He pointed to a gold ring in the floor. He asked me what I thought. I shrugged. He bent, all bones like an ortolan, and pulled on it: trapdoor. He got a board from a smouldering pile in the corner and rubbed a rag onto it to make it hot. He led me on.

When I was a waiter I likely served their parents. Perhaps I suggested, while knowing my place, the wine that served as the aphrodisiac spark of their getting. I was a waiter in some fine establishments, you see, in some of the finest establishments, and just today when I stopped to pick up a good long rectangle of corrugated cardboard for bedding I thought of myself, in black bow tie, waltzing through the dining room with a bowl of walnut scented gnocchi, peerless. My clients, my clients would ask the maitre d' for me, especially. They took the same table each Friday evening. The wallpaper was embossed cream. Now their children beat me with broom handles. Though we believed in the same Gods. We were dying out then, we were all dying out; but I remember a white-faced Duchess pulling me down towards her, gripping my forearm, for dear life, to whisper: *Charles!* And she would ask me: what do you know of the God with the butler? Such might be her concerns. The God they put on trial, have you heard anything? My clients, my clients knew that I had been a priest, hundreds of thousands of years before, and though it might seem socially awkward – or politically awkward, given the times – to ask, such was their devotion that they did ask. People with true manners can break the rules, from time to time, *because they do so with grace.*

The boys live in tents in the vacant lots. They shit in rubble and eat cats. Memory is the gouger and memory is the salve. I sing to the God of foolishness as I walk, I joke with the God who murdered the old washerwoman. The boys wear bandanas and carry knives. They scream out scurrilous threats to my manhood, such as it is. I look for cans of food, and there are places where you will be given fetid soup. And there are people trying to be good, who wish to share, who will not send you away, at least until they tire of you. Sometimes I sit in my cart, when it is raining. I push myself under an awning and lick the washy rills off my cheeks, they taste of arse. Sometimes I collect enough bottles to trade in for a delicious hot dog. Bubbles of grease collecting into lines. As I walk I keep my eye on the building pediments and I see the Gods perched on the roofs like hawks.

We were in one of the oldest temples. A place that was ancient before ancient things were conceived of. Murky air, the Egyptian smell, and sneaker and boot-prints in the thick white dust. And we could feel the stone jut so slightly out where once there had been wood panels; my hopes welled again. How cold it was! Something moved against a wall to terrify me. My boy waved his torch at it. The God of eels. I was full of the past: I could see acolytes kneeling in a row, I could think our rites were performed here, and here, and here, a million years ago. Tears welling? I wanted to thank him: me, thank a boy, for bringing me to this place. The priest thanks the ephebe: all that is solid melts into air. He went away to the right; I regretted us making any noise at all, here, I breathed in our scent. His thin shoulders, the two of us in the crypt: Sandro and I in the wine cellars, the night I was fired. Then in the dark, in the burning shadows, he showed me a golden bird – and I lost my breath. We were silent. It is a great and powerful God, I murmured, unsure of myself, unsure of my judgment. Can it do anything, he asked me. His yellow and black smiling mouth. He said: I knew you'd tell us if it was worth anything.

My position had become if not unsafe then at least unsavoury. There was a sense of the best of times having passed. The Gods had sanctified my clients; the Gods had layered the world into sponge and icing. What mulch would follow their departure? My clients were anxious. I leaned in closer. Whispering, quickly, so as not to be seen: The Gods cannot be harmed, I told the wealthy. Do you think the God of the twenty-four hours is mortal? The God of cunning tribes persists, I told them. Full of hope they would watch me roll out the desserts.

When I was a priest I caressed these heads. I trained them. I was a man in charge of boys. I took my work seriously because I knew that I was one of a long line, and I knew that these boys would one day become men, and would need a code and an order tucked inside them, a map gradually unfurling in the esophagus. I led them in rites and songs, their parents trusted me. Parents brought me their most prized possessions, their boys. They came to my temple and left them with me with a solitary instruction: Mould this wet lump into a man.

One of the boys has curly hair. Another's locks are lank and soft as an otter blanket. One of the boys has studs in his eyelid, this is something I do not condone. Mine is a soft one, he is less of a criminal. When the five of them chase me down the alley and kick my cart over and stamp my bedding into icy puddles and try to set fire to my cart and leave me bashed and bleeding, I sometimes feel he is acting more half-heartedly than the rest, or at least thinking of hanging back. I focus on him, his gritted teeth. If you had come into the Doré I'd have brought you a strawberry nectar. Not from the menu; something special from André, especially for the young master. Say this to yourself as you count your teeth with your cut tongue and scream. On the journey home, after dropping him back at school, the mother would say to the father: what a good, kind man Charles is. We must remember him at Christmas. And the father, sitting behind the driver, nods. The same quick nod as his boy. Reading the editorial page. With half a sirloin for the young master. Half a steak for the God of half steaks. I tell him about the God of flight. I sit in the sun and sing and fart: the Gods pray to *Me*.

When the policemen last brought me in, they fed me gruel; my cell mates beat me with the plastic tray. So the policemen kept me apart. They had their orderlies wash me and so I saw my privates. They gave me a new pair of pyjamas. The inspector was a woman. I came about, I came to, they sat me in a chair. She told me that the problem was not that they could not find the perpetrators; what I was describing was not considered a crime at all. So she had no choice but to let me go.

Three times until it came he wrenched at the bird and then lifted it off the wall. He brought it to the dusty table we'd pulled into the middle of the room. The boy stepped back, and so I began, knowing that I was full with the God. And if I did not remember the precise detail in its precise configuration, still I was in the place with the altar and the wafer and the helping hand. I moved my hands across the bird. I spoke to the winking God of Deathbed Renunciation. I broke off. I told the boy: we perform the rite to step into the God's world, away from our own. We must needs be calm, if we are to succeed. It is best done at nightfall, I told him, but here we can forget both the sun and the moon. He spat on the floor. What's a rite, he asked me. I began again; I moved my hands over the bird and said what words I could. Here was sweat on my forehead, sweat in this cold place. I thought I saw the bird spread its wings but it stayed where it was. The boy was playing: he rested his knife blade on the ripped fabric over his thigh, I could see the naked skin in the torchlight. I said to the boy: come closer, I need you, I need you to help me.

Mice whistle at me in the nighttime, they bite my scalp. But how can I send them away? They smirk at me from restaurant windows. It is hard to maintain the rituals. The boys have their own Gods now. But why must it be so hard to think, to recall? Especially if I am a cupbearer, as I think I am. What is lacking in me now is clarity of spirit. One must be able to think, if one is to pray. The Gods require attention, when things things things of the world bustle in. I mean crows perched on rotting telegraph poles, I mean an empty chariot, I mean that I can hardly recall the duties I owe to the God of guides or the God of form. Hail scatters down on glass, though there are no clouds. Do you remember I found this cart a block from a supermarket? It is mine. I wiped myself on your newspaper. Help me to persist.

Know what I think, he asked me. I had my hands at my sides. How can I plant where there is no soil? You want to know what I think. I was watching the bird. He said: You're a dirty filthy old man, aren't you. You're a dirty filthy horrible old man, that's what I think. I was looking at the bird. You brought me down here to have your wicked way with me, didn't you. Brought me down to your hole because you like to finger little boys, don't you. You like to poke your finger in. I heard steps, I saw figures approaching, but I knew that the God of tight corners would protect me. I mumbled the words.

I tried to tell them what a God is, I told them about the wind and the rain. They wanted drugs. They encircled me, smelling of warfare, twiddling their knives. I thought they might like the God of travelling across the country with only one shirt. Their faces perked up a little and they made jokes about rape and pushed at me. I started to falter: did the God carry his own spear or was it his dear friend's? I was lost: walking through an abandoned house, your foot crashes through the floor boards. They could see it. This is a God, I said to them, with my hands far apart; but it used to be our God. I was thinking of the God of hermaphroditism. I said: Now it is my God. We have the treatment, my boy said. A God is made by rite and prayer, I said. Do you know what rite and prayer means? The Gods used to come to men at nightfall, I said, by the evening lamp, I said again. We have the treatment for dirty old men, he said. They used to whisper. Threatening murmurs, gobs of snot spitting at my feet. I waited for the God of steaming or the God of money to come and tell me.

We have the treatment for dirty filthy old men. We do. Five of them now, faces sweaty, smirking, they were coming closer. We have the treatment. They set about me with brass on their hands. With the first blow I tottered; the pain in my jaw and my neck and shoulder, it made me think of the God who withstood everything. The first kick in my groin clenched me double. Going down I saw the bird, would they use it on me as a weapon, I thought; but they had weapons of their own. Dirty, filthy, they were chanting. I was lying on the floor, they kicked me onto my side and onto my back and onto my front, my organs protested, the vomit filled my bloody mouth. My eye disappeared into its own jelly. I made no effort to protect myself: the God of the soul clenched between your teeth.

Carolyn Black is a Toronto writer whose work has appeared in *EVENT*, *Exile*, *The New Quarterly*, and *Room*. Her story "Thirty-Seven Women" can be read online at Joyland.ca. "Serial Love" is part of a completed manuscript of short stories about the body in peril.

Andrew Boden's stories and essays have recently appeared in *Descant*, *Vancouver Review*, *Other Voices*, *Storyteller*, and the anthologies *Nobody's Father: Life Without Kids* and *The Best of Every Day Fiction Two*. He is currently working on a novel and co-editing a collection of personal essays about mental illness. He lives and works in Burnaby, British Columbia.

Laura Boudreau is a graduate of the University of Toronto's M.A. in English in the Field of Creative Writing program. Her fiction has appeared in a variety of Canadian literary journals, including *The New Quarterly*, *Grain*, and *The Fiddlehead*, and is forthcoming in *10: Best Canadian Stories* from Oberon Press. "The Dead Dad Game" previously won *PRISM international*'s Short Fiction Contest. Her first collection of stories will be published by Biblioasis in 2011.

Devon Code is from Dartmouth, Nova Scotia. His story collection, *In a Mist* (Invisible Publishing, 2007), was chosen by the *Globe and Mail* as a notable fiction debut of 2008. For the last three years, he has served as a writer-in-residence with the Toronto Catholic District School Board as part of the Now Hear This! S.W.A.T. program. He lives in Toronto.

Danielle Egan is a Vancouver-based writer and journalist. Her non-fiction has been nominated for National and Western Magazine Awards and she has published short fiction in *Taddle Creek*, *Maisonneuve*, *Vancouver Review*, and *Joyland*.

Krista Foss has published fiction in *Grain*, *The Antigonish Review*, *Room*, and *EVENT*. Her first published short story was a finalist for the 2007 Journey Prize. She is currently working on her M.F.A. in Creative Writing at the University of British Columbia's Optional Residency program. She is a proud denizen of Hamilton, Ontario.

Lynne Kutsukake's short fiction has appeared in *The Dalhousie Review*, *Grain*, *The Windsor Review*, *Ricepaper*, and *Prairie Fire*. One of her stories was anthologized in last year's volume of *The Journey Prize Stories*. She is currently completing a collection of short stories and is hard at work on a novel. She lives in Toronto.

Ben Lof has published fiction in *The Malahat Review* and *Prairie Fire*, and he was a finalist for the 2007 RBC Bronwen Wallace Award for Emerging Writers. He is a graduate of the University of Alberta with an M.A. in English, and lives in Edmonton, where he is completing a short fiction manuscript. "When in the Field with Her at His Back" won the 2010 Howard O'Hagan Award for Short Story.

Andrew MacDonald has an M.A. in English in the Field of Creative Writing from the University of Toronto. His stories and reviews have been published in places like *EVENT*, *The Fiddlehead*, *Existere*, *Feathertale*, and *Broken Pencil*. He lives with tuxedo cats in Toronto, where he's writing more stories and a novel.

Eliza Robertson is finishing her undergraduate degree in Creative Writing and Political Science at the University of Victoria. "Ship's Log" was her first published story and won *The Malahat Review*'s 2009 Far Horizons Contest. In the past year she has also won the short story contests for *The Fiddlehead* and *PRISM international*.

Mike Spry is a writer and editor living in Montreal. His work has appeared in *Matrix*, *This Magazine*, *Geist*, and *filling Station*, among others. His collection of poetry, *JACK* (Snare Books, 2008), was shortlisted for the Quebec Writers' Federation's A.M. Klein Prize for Poetry.

Damian Tarnopolsky is the author of *Lanzmann and Other Stories*, a widely praised collection of short fiction, and the novel *Goya's Dog*, which was shortlisted for the Commonwealth Writers' Prize (Canada and Caribbean region) and the Amazon.ca First Novel Award. His stories have been published in *Maisonneuve*, *Exile*, and *subTerrain*, and have been shortlisted for the CBC Literary Award and the ReLit Award. His story "Sleepy" appeared in *The Journey Prize Anthology 18*. He lives in Toronto with his family and is at work on two new novels.

ABOUT THE CONTRIBUTING JOURNALS

For more information about all the journals that submitted stories to this year's anthology, please consult *The Journey Prize Stories* website: www.mcclelland.com/jps.

The Dalhousie Review has been in operation since 1921 and aspires to be a forum in which seriousness of purpose and playfulness of mind can coexist in meaningful dialogue. The journal publishes new fiction and poetry in every issue and welcomes submissions from authors around the world. Editor: Anthony Stewart. Submissions and correspondence: *The Dalhousie Review*, Dalhousie University, Halifax, Nova Scotia, B3H 4R2. Email: dalhousie.review@dal.ca Website: www.dalhousiereview.dal.ca

EVENT is a celebrated literary journal showcasing new and established talent – in fiction, poetry, non-fiction, and critical reviews. The journal thrives on a balance of both traditional narrative and contemporary approaches to poetry and prose. *EVENT* is home to Canada's longest-running annual non-fiction contest. It is our goal to support and encourage a thriving literary community in Canada, while maintaining our international reputation for excellence. Editor: Elizabeth Bachinsky. Managing Editor: Ian Cockfield. Fiction Editor: Christine Dewar. Submissions and correspondence: *EVENT*, P.O. Box 2503, New Westminster, British Columbia,

V3L 5B2. Email (queries only): event@douglas.bc.ca Website:
http://event.douglas.bc.ca

Exile: The Literary Quarterly is a distinctive journal that
offers a rich and varied selection of new, emerging, and established writers of fiction, poetry, excerpts in translation, and
drama, and features artists working in a wide range of
mediums. With over one thousand contributions since 1972,
Exile draws material from French and English Canada, as well
as from the United States, Britain, Europe, Latin America,
the Middle East, and Asia. Publisher: Michael Callaghan.
Editor-in-Chief: Barry Callaghan. Submissions and correspondence: Exile/Excelsior Publishing Inc., 134 Eastbourne
Avenue, Toronto, Ontario, M5P 2G6. Email (queries only):
exq@exilequarterly.com Website: www.exilequarterly.com

Grain Magazine, a literary quarterly, publishes engaging, sur-
prising, eclectic, and challenging writing and art by Canadian
and international writers and artists. Published by the
Saskatchewan Writers Guild, *Grain* has earned national and
international recognition for its distinctive content. Editor:
Sylvia Legris. Submissions and correspondence: *Grain
Magazine*, P.O. Box 67, Saskatoon, Saskatchewan, S7K 3K1.
Email: grainmag@sasktel.net Website: www.grainmagazine.ca

The Malahat Review is a quarterly journal of contemporary
poetry, fiction, and creative non-fiction by both new and celebrated writers. Summer issues feature the winners of
Malahat's Novella and Long Poem prizes, held in alternate

years; the fall issues feature the winners of the Far Horizons Award for emerging writers, alternating between poetry and fiction each year; the winter issues feature the winners of the Creative Non-Fiction Prize; and beginning in 2010, the spring issues will feature winners from the Open Season Awards in all three genres (poetry, fiction, and creative non-fiction). All issues feature covers by noted Canadian visual artists and include reviews of Canadian books. Editor: John Barton. Assistant Editor: Rhonda Batchelor. Submissions and correspondence: *The Malahat Review*, University of Victoria, P.O. Box 1700, Station csc, Victoria, British Columbia, V8W 2Y2. Email: malahat@uvic.ca Website: www.malahatreview.ca

PRISM international, the oldest literary magazine in Western Canada, was established in 1959 by a group of Vancouver writers. Published four times a year, *PRISM* features short fiction, poetry, creative non-fiction, and translations by both new and established writers from Canada and around the world. The only criteria are originality and quality. *PRISM* holds four exemplary competitions: the Short Fiction Contest, the Literary Non-fiction Contest, the Poetry Contest, and the Earle Birney Prize for Poetry. Executive Editors: Ben Rawluk and Chris Urquhart. Fiction Editor: Jeff Stautz. Poetry Editor: andrea bennett. Submissions and correspondence: *PRISM international*, Creative Writing Program, The University of British Columbia, Buchanan E-462, 1866 Main Mall, Vancouver, British Columbia, V6T 1Z1. Email (for queries only): prism@interchange.ubc.ca Website: www.prismmagazine.ca

subTerrain Magazine publishes contemporary and some-times controversial Canadian fiction, poetry, non-fiction, and visual art. Every issue features interviews, timely commentary, and book reviews. Praised by both writers and readers for fea-turing work that might not find a home in more conservative periodicals, *subTerrain* seeks to expand the definition of Canadian literary and artistic culture by showcasing the best in progressive writing and ideas. Please visit our website for more information on upcoming theme issues, our annual Lush Triumphant contest, general submission guidelines, and subscription information. Submissions and correspondence: *subTerrain Magazine*, P.O. Box 3008, MPO, Vancouver, British Columbia, V6B 3X5. Website: www.subterrain.ca

For more than four decades, **This Magazine** has proudly pub-lished fiction and poetry from new and emerging Canadian writers. A sassy and thoughtful journal of arts, politics, and pop culture, *This* consistently offers fresh takes on familiar issues, as well as breaking stories that need to be told. Publisher: Lisa Whittington-Hill. Fiction & Poetry Editor: Stuart Ross. Correspondence: *This Magazine*, Suite 396 – 401 Richmond Ave. W., Toronto, Ontario, M5V 3A8. Website: this.org

Vancouver Review is an iconoclastic, irreverent, and wholly independent cultural quarterly that celebrated its fifth anniver-sary in 2009. *Vancouver Review* focuses on B.C. cultural, social, and political issues, and publishes commentary, essays, and nar-rative non-fiction, as well as fiction and poetry in every issue. With its Blueprint B.C. Fiction Series, launched in the summer of 2007, it explores the zeitgeist and geographic implications of the province through illustrated stories by first-time and established authors. Editor: Gudrun Will. Fiction Editor: Zsuzsi Gartner. Poetry Editor: Caroline Harvey. Submissions and correspondence (email submissions preferred): *Vancouver Review*, 2828 West 13th Avenue, Vancouver, British Columbia, V6K 2T7. Email: editor@vancouverreview.com Website: www.vancouverreview.com

Submissions were also received from the following journals:

The Antigonish Review
(Antigonish, N.S.)
www.antigonishreview.com

The Claremont Review
(Victoria, B.C.)
www.theclaremontreview.ca

Ars Medica
(Toronto, Ont.)
www.utpjournals.com/ars/ars
.html

Descant
(Toronto, Ont.)
www.descant.ca

The Fiddlehead
(Fredericton, N.B.)
www.thefiddlehead.ca

Brick
(Toronto, Ont.)
www.brickmag.com

FreeFall Magazine
(Calgary, Alta.)
www.freefallmagazine.ca

Broken Pencil
(Toronto, Ont.)
www.brokenpencil.com

Geist
(Vancouver, B.C.)
www.geist.com

carte blanche
(Westmount, Que.)
www.carte-blanche.org

Joyland
(Toronto, Ont.)
www.joyland.ca

Matrix Magazine
(Montreal, Que.)
www.matrixmagazine.org

The New Orphic Review
(Nelson, B.C.)
www3.telus.net/neworphicpu
blishers-hekkanen

The New Quarterly
(Waterloo, Ont.)
www.tnq.ca

On Spec
(Edmonton, Alta.)
www.onspec.ca

Pilot Illustrated Magazine
(Toronto, Ont.)
www.thepilotproject.ca

Prairie Fire
(Winnipeg, Man.)
www.prairiefire.ca

The Prairie Journal
(Calgary, Alta.)
www.prairiejournal.org

Queen's Quarterly
(Kingston, Ont.)
www.queensu.ca/quarterly

Riddle Fence
(St. John's, NL)
www.riddlefence.com

Room Magazine
(Vancouver, B.C.)
www.roommagazine.com

Taddle Creek
(Toronto, Ont.)
www.taddlecreekmag.com

PREVIOUS CONTRIBUTING AUTHORS

* Winners of the $10,000 Journey Prize

** Co-winners of the $10,000 Journey Prize

I

1989

SELECTED WITH ALISTAIR MacLEOD

Ven Begamudré, "Word Games"

David Bergen, "Where You're From"

Lois Braun, "The Pumpkin-Eaters"

Constance Buchanan, "Man with Flying Genitals"

Ann Copeland, "Obedience"

Marion Douglas, "Flags"

Frances Itani, "An Evening in the Café"

Diane Keating, "The Crying Out"

Thomas King, "One Good Story, That One"

Holley Rubinsky, "Rapid Transits"*

Jean Rysstad, "Winter Baby"

Kevin Van Tighem, "Whoopers"

M.G. Vassanji, "In the Quiet of a Sunday Afternoon"

Bronwen Wallace, "Chicken 'N' Ribs"

Armin Wiebe, "Mouse Lake"

Budge Wilson, "Waiting"

2

1990

SELECTED WITH LEON ROOKE; GUY VANDERHAEGHE

André Alexis, "Despair: Five Stories of Ottawa"

Glen Allen, "The Hua Guofeng Memorial Warehouse"

Marusia Bociurkiw, "Mama, Donya"

Virgil Burnett, "Billfrith the Dreamer"

Margaret Dyment, "Sacred Trust"

Cynthia Flood, "My Father Took a Cake to France"*

Douglas Glover, "Story Carved in Stone"

Terry Griggs, "Man with the Axe"

Rick Hillis, "Limbo River"

Thomas King, "The Dog I Wish I Had, I Would Call It Helen"

K.D. Miller, "Sunrise Till Dark"

Jennifer Mitton, "Let Them Say"

Lawrence O'Toole, "Goin' to Town with Katie Ann"

Kenneth Radu, "A Change of Heart"

Jenifer Sutherland, "Table Talk"

Wayne Tefs, "Red Rock and After"

3

1991

SELECTED WITH JANE URQUHART

Donald Aker, "The Invitation"

Anton Baer, "Yukon"

Allan Barr, "A Visit from Lloyd"

David Bergen, "The Fall"

Rai Berzins, "Common Sense"

Diana Hartog, "Theories of Grief"

Diane Keating, "The Salem Letters"

Yann Martel, "The Facts Behind the Helsinki Roccamatios"*

Jennifer Mitton, "Polaroid"

Sheldon Oberman, "This Business with Elijah"

Lynn Podgurny, "Till Tomorrow, Maple Leaf Mills"

James Riseborough, "She Is Not His Mother"

Patricia Stone, "Living on the Lake"

4

1992

SELECTED WITH SANDRA BIRDSELL

David Bergen, "The Bottom of the Glass"

Maria A. Billion, "No Miracles Sweet Jesus"

Judith Cowan, "By the Big River"

Steven Heighton, "A Man Away from Home Has No Neighbours"

Steven Heighton, "How Beautiful upon the Mountains"

L. Rex Kay, "Travelling"

Rozena Maart, "No Rosa, No District Six"*

Guy Malet De Carteret, "Rainy Day"

Carmelita McGrath, "Silence"

Michael Mirolla, "A Theory of Discontinuous Existence"

Diane Juttner Perreault, "Bella's Story"

Eden Robinson, "Traplines"

5

1993

SELECTED WITH GUY VANDERHAEGHE

Caroline Adderson, "Oil and Dread"

David Bergen, "La Rue Prevette"

Marina Endicott, "With the Band"

Dayv James-French, "Cervine"

Michael Kenyon, "Durable Tumblers"

K.D. Miller, "A Litany in Time of Plague"

Robert Mullen, "Flotsam"

Gayla Reid, "Sister Doyle's Men"*

Oakland Ross, "Bang-bang"

Robert Sherrin, "Technical Battle for Trial Machine"

Carol Windley, "The Etruscans"

6

1994

SELECTED WITH DOUGLAS GLOVER;

JUDITH CHANT (CHAPTERS)

Anne Carson, "Water Margins: An Essay on Swimming by My Brother"

Richard Cumyn, "The Sound He Made"

Genni Gunn, "Versions"

Melissa Hardy, "Long Man the River"*

Robert Mullen, "Anomie"

Vivian Payne, "Free Falls"

Jim Reil, "Dry"

Robyn Sarah, "Accept My Story"

Joan Skogan, "Landfall"

Dorothy Speak, "Relatives in Florida"

Alison Wearing, "Notes from Under Water"

7

1995

SELECTED WITH M.G. VASSANJI;

RICHARD BACHMANN (A DIFFERENT DRUMMER BOOKS)

Michelle Alfano, "Opera"

Mary Borsky, "Maps of the Known World"

Gabriella Goliger, "Song of Ascent"

Elizabeth Hay, "Hand Games"

Shaena Lambert, "The Falling Woman"

Elise Levine, "Boy"

Roger Burford Mason, "The Rat-Catcher's Kiss"

Antanas Sileika, "Going Native"

Kathryn Woodward, "Of Marranos and Gilded Angels"*

8

1996

SELECTED WITH OLIVE SENIOR;

BEN McNALLY (NICHOLAS HOARE LTD.)

Rick Bowers, "Dental Bytes"

David Elias, "How I Crossed Over"

Elyse Gasco, "Can You Wave Bye Bye, Baby?"*

Danuta Gleed, "Bones"

Elizabeth Hay, "The Friend"

Linda Holeman, "Turning the Worm"

Elaine Littman, "The Winner's Circle"

Murray Logan, "Steam"

Rick Maddocks, "Lessons from the Sputnik Diner"

K.D. Miller, "Egypt Land"

Gregor Robinson, "Monster Gaps"

Alma Subasic, "Dust"

9

1997

SELECTED WITH NINO RICCI; NICHOLAS PASHLEY

(UNIVERSITY OF TORONTO BOOKSTORE)

Brian Bartlett, "Thomas, Naked"

Dennis Bock, "Olympia"

Kristen den Hartog, "Wave"

Gabriella Goliger, "Maladies of the Inner Ear"**

Terry Griggs, "Momma Had a Baby"

Mark Anthony Jarman, "Righteous Speedboat"

Judith Kalman, "Not for Me a Crown of Thorns"

Andrew Mullins, "The World of Science"

Sasenarine Persaud, "Canada Geese and Apple Chatney"

Anne Simpson, "Dreaming Snow"**

Sarah Withrow, "Ollie"

Terence Young, "The Berlin Wall"

10

1998

SELECTED BY PETER BUITENHUIS; HOLLEY RUBINSKY;

CELIA DUTHIE (DUTHIE BOOKS LTD.)

John Brooke, "The Finer Points of Apples"*

Ian Colford, "The Reason for the Dream"

Libby Creelman, "Cruelty"

Michael Crummey, "Serendipity"

Stephen Guppy, "Downwind"

Jane Eaton Hamilton, "Graduation"

Elise Levine, "You Are You Because Your Little Dog Loves You"

Jean McNeil, "Bethlehem"

Liz Moore, "Eight-Day Clock"

Edward O'Connor, "The Beatrice of Victoria College"

Tim Rogers, "Scars and Other Presents"

Denise Ryan, "Marginals, Vivisections, and Dreams"

Madeleine Thien, "Simple Recipes"

Cheryl Tibbetts, "Flowers of Africville"

11

1999

SELECTED BY LESLEY CHOYCE; SHELDON CURRIE;

MARY-JO ANDERSON (FROG HOLLOW BOOKS)

Mike Barnes, "In Florida"

Libby Creelman, "Sunken Island"

Mike Finigan, "Passion Sunday"

Jane Eaton Hamilton, "Territory"

Mark Anthony Jarman, "Travels into Several Remote Nations of the
  World"

Barbara Lambert, "Where the Bodies Are Kept"

Linda Little, "The Still"

Larry Lynch, "The Sitter"

Sandra Sabatini, "The One With the News"

Sharon Steams, "Brothers"

Mary Walters, "Show Jumping"

Alissa York, "The Back of the Bear's Mouth"*

12

2000

SELECTED BY CATHERINE BUSH; HAL NIEDZVIECKI;

MARC GLASSMAN (PAGES BOOKS AND MAGAZINES)

Andrew Gray, "The Heart of the Land"

Lee Henderson, "Sheep Dub"

Jessica Johnson, "We Move Slowly"

John Lavery, "The Premier's New Pyjamas"

J.A. McCormack, "Hearsay"

Nancy Richler, "Your Mouth Is Lovely"

Andrew Smith, "Sightseeing"

Karen Solie, "Onion Calendar"

Timothy Taylor, "Doves of Townsend"*

Timothy Taylor, "Pope's Own"

Timothy Taylor, "Silent Cruise"

R.M. Vaughan, "Swan Street"

13

2001

SELECTED BY ELYSE GASCO; MICHAEL HELM;

MICHAEL NICHOLSON (INDIGO BOOKS & MUSIC INC.)

Kevin Armstrong, "The Cane Field"*

Mike Barnes, "Karaoke Mon Amour"

Heather Birrell, "Machaya"

Heather Birrell, "The Present Perfect"

Craig Boyko, "The Gun"

Vivette J. Kady, "Anything That Wiggles"

Billie Livingston, "You're Taking All the Fun Out of It"

Annabel Lyon, "Fishes"

Lisa Moore, "The Way the Light Is"

Heather O'Neill, "Little Suitcase"

Susan Rendell, "In the Chambers of the Sea"

Tim Rogers, "Watch"

Margrith Schraner, "Dream Dig"

14

2002

SELECTED BY ANDRÉ ALEXIS;

DEREK McCORMACK; DIANE SCHOEMPERLEN

Mike Barnes, "Cogagwee"

Geoffrey Brown, "Listen"

Jocelyn Brown, "Miss Canada"*

Emma Donoghue, "What Remains"

Jonathan Goldstein, "You Are a Spaceman With Your Head Under the Bathroom Stall Door"

Robert McGill, "Confidence Men"

Robert McGill, "The Stars Are Falling"

Nick Melling, "Philemon"

Robert Mullen, "Alex the God"

Karen Munro, "The Pool"

Leah Postman, "Being Famous"

Neil Smith, "Green Fluorescent Protein"

15

2003

SELECTED BY MICHELLE BERRY;

TIMOTHY TAYLOR; MICHAEL WINTER

Rosaria Campbell, "Reaching"

Hilary Dean, "The Lemon Stories"

Dawn Rae Downton, "Hansel and Gretel"

Anne Fleming, "Gay Dwarves of America"

Elyse Friedman, "Truth"

Charlotte Gill, "Hush"

Jessica Grant, "My Husband's Jump"*

Jacqueline Honnet, "Conversion Classes"

S.K. Johannesen, "Resurrection"

Avner Mandelman, "Cuckoo"

Tim Mitchell, "Night Finds Us"

Heather O'Neill, "The Difference Between Me and Goldstein"

16

2004

SELECTED BY ELIZABETH HAY;

LISA MOORE; MICHAEL REDHILL

Anar Ali, "Baby Khaki's Wings"

Kenneth Bonert, "Packers and Movers"

Jennifer Clouter, "Benny and the Jets"

Daniel Griffin, "Mercedes Buyer's Guide"

Michael Kissinger, "Invest in the North"

Devin Krukoff, "The Last Spark"*

Elaine McCluskey, "The Watermelon Social"

William Metcalfe, "Nice Big Car, Rap Music Coming
   Out the Window"

Lesley Millard, "The Uses of the Neckerchief"

Adam Lewis Schroeder, "Burning the Cattle at Both Ends"

Michael V. Smith, "What We Wanted"

Neil Smith, "Isolettes"

Patricia Rose Young, "Up the Clyde on a Bike"

17

2005

SELECTED BY JAMES GRAINGER AND NANCY LEE

Randy Boyagoda, "Rice and Curry Yacht Club"

Krista Bridge, "A Matter of Firsts"

Josh Byer, "Rats, Homosex, Saunas, and Simon"

Craig Davidson, "Failure to Thrive"

McKinley M. Hellenes, "Brighter Thread"

Catherine Kidd, "Green-Eyed Beans"

Pasha Malla, "The Past Composed"

Edward O'Connor, "Heard Melodies Are Sweet"

Barbara Romanik, "Seven Ways into Chandigarh"

Sandra Sabatini, "The Dolphins at Sainte Marie"

Matt Shaw, "Matchbook for a Mother's Hair"*

Richard Simas, "Anthropologies"

Neil Smith, "Scrapbook"

Emily White, "Various Metals"

18

2006

SELECTED BY STEVEN GALLOWAY;

ZSUZSI GARTNER; ANNABEL LYON

Heather Birrell, "BriannaSusannaAlana"*

Craig Boyko, "The Baby"

Craig Boyko, "The Beloved Departed"

Nadia Bozak, "Heavy Metal Housekeeping"

Lee Henderson, "Conjugation"

Melanie Little, "Wrestling"

Matthew Rader, "The Lonesome Death of Joseph Fey"

Scott Randall, "Law School"

Sarah Selecky, "Throwing Cotton"

Damian Tarnopolsky, "Sleepy"

Martin West, "Cretacea"

David Whitton, "The Eclipse"

Clea Young, "Split"

19

2007

SELECTED BY CAROLINE ADDERSON;

DAVID BEZMOZGIS; DIONNE BRAND

Andrew J. Borkowski, "Twelve Versions of Lech"

Craig Boyko, "OZY"*

Grant Buday, "The Curve of the Earth"

Nicole Dixon, "High-water Mark"

Krista Foss, "Swimming in Zanzibar"

Pasha Malla, "Respite"

Alice Petersen, "After Summer"

Patricia Robertson, "My Hungarian Sister"

Rebecca Rosenblum, "Chilly Girl"

Nicholas Ruddock, "How Eunice Got Her Baby"

Jean Van Loon, "Stardust"

20

2008

SELECTED BY LYNN COADY;

HEATHER O'NEILL; NEIL SMITH

Théodora Armstrong, "Whale Stories"

Mike Christie, "Goodbye Porkpie Hat"

Anna Leventhal, "The Polar Bear at the Museum"

Naomi K. Lewis, "The Guiding Light"

Oscar Martens, "Breaking on the Wheel"

Dana Mills, "Steaming for Godthab"

Saleema Nawaz, "My Three Girls"*

Scott Randall, "The Gifted Class"

S. Kennedy Sobol, "Some Light Down"

Sarah Steinberg, "At Last at Sea"

Clea Young, "Chaperone"

21

2009

SELECTED BY CAMILLA GIBB;

LEE HENDERSON; REBECCA ROSENBLUM

Daniel Griffin, "The Last Great Works of Alvin Cale"

Jesus Hardwell, "Easy Living"

Paul Headrick, "Highlife"

Sarah Keevil, "Pyro"

Adrian Michael Kelly, "Lure"

Fran Kimmel, "Picturing God's Ocean"

Lynne Kutsukake, "Away"

Alexander MacLeod, "Miracle Mile"

Dave Margoshes, "The Wisdom of Solomon"

Shawn Syms, "On the Line"

Sarah L. Taggart, "Deaf"

Yasuko Thanh, "Floating Like the Dead"*